The Storm Blitz

Lane Walker

LOCAL LEGENDS
www.bakkenbooks.com

ISBN 978-1-955657-37-2
For Worldwide Distribution
Printed in the U.S.A.

Published by Bakken Books
2022
www.bakkenbooks.com

*This book is dedicated to
all those who learned from their mistakes,
improving themselves through all the storms and
challenges of life.*

Local Legends

The Buzzer Beater

The High Cheese

The Storm Blitz

Coming Soon!

Local Legends — Golf

Local Legends — Soccer

Hometown Hunters Collection

Legend of the Ghost Buck

The Hunt for Scarface

Terror on Deadwood Lake

The Boss on Redemption Road

The Day It Rained Ducks

The Lost Deer Camp

The Fishing Chronicles

Monster of Farallon Islands

The River King

The Ice Queen

The Bass Factory

The Search for Big Lou

For more books, visit: **www.bakkenbooks.com**

-1-

Prologue

My dad always told me never to worry about things that had already happened and to let the past be the past.

"Bruno, you can't always look in the rearview mirror. That's why it's so much smaller than the windshield. You have to look ahead to forget about the past," he would say.

Today, I was looking ahead.

I was staring directly in the eyes of the Seaside Mustangs All-American quarterback, Jacoby Howard.

Even though Jacoby was only in eighth grade, he already stood 6'2" and weighed over 170 pounds.

He was enormous compared to most of his teammates. But his size wasn't even his best attribute.

Jacoby was lightning quick, recognized as one of the fastest eighth graders in the state of Florida.

The stories about him embarrassing opposing players echoed throughout the local playgrounds and streamed through social media. Ever since I was in fourth grade, I had heard amazing tales about his football ability.

He was so fast he was beating sixth graders in races when he was only in second grade. He had never lost a race in track—ever!

The Mustang quarterback already looked poised to be all-state in high school, go to a Division 1 (D-1) college and become a future NFL star.

Howard could run and throw; this season alone he had gained 1,700 yards without receiving a pass, rushing 200+ yards in multiple games.

But today, he didn't need hundreds of yards.

He only needed a few inches.

It was fourth and goal, and Jacoby had the ball inches away from the goal line.

We held a 21-17 lead over the Mustangs—a team we had never beaten and one that hadn't lost a game in over four years.

Fourth down...

The Mustangs used their last time out. I glanced up at the play clock; it read :03. All that stood in front of Howard was our aggressive South Bay Shark defense.

This play would be one I would remember forever; after all, it was for everything.

Our teams were both 8-0, and we had dominated all the other teams we had played. Not only was this the last game of the season; only one winner would be crowned the king of Panama City Middle School football.

Sweat poured into my eyes, creating an achy, fiery sensation. I didn't mind it; in fact, I liked the burn. I tried my best not to flinch or blink. I didn't want Jacoby to see any weakness in me when his eyes met mine. My glare was straight and intentional.

He was the star quarterback, and I was the middle

linebacker who was going to stop him from scoring. I wanted him to feel like the end zone was a thousand miles away. Confidently, Howard winked at me as he approached his offensive line to call the cadence for the last play of the game.

My body stiffened and straightened as I barked to my defensive teammates, "Not today, boys! Not even an inch—not today!"

The huge crowd fell silent, and I was alone with my thoughts.

"Who does this Jacoby Howard think he is?" I asked myself. He knew we weren't intimated by his mastery of the game or in awe of him. He was great, but so were we. I had spent my entire summer training for this one moment—the chance to knock off the Seaside Mustangs and secure bragging rights for the Sharks.

My teeth clenched as I dropped into the classic three-point stance playing my defensive position. I felt invincible. After everything we had been through the past four weeks, I knew there was no way he was going to get into the end zone.

I was going to meet him head on, directly in the hole.

I was the brick wall.

Jacoby had to go through me to win the game.

That isn't going to happen.

"Could one play really make that much of a difference?"

This is my moment. I knew it was now or never.

This wasn't like any other fourth down in the history of Shark football. This one play could make us the first undefeated team in South Bay history.

Even though this was a junior-high football game, it meant so much more.

In my mind it wasn't fourth and one, it was fourth and forever!

-2-

"Bruno, keep your head up! You can't hit what you can't see," my dad bellowed during a tackling drill on the first day of football practice in early August.

I was lucky. My dad had been my football coach since I had started playing tackle football in the third grade. He was a diehard football fan and an amazing football player when he was younger. Dad had attended a small Division 2 college in Michigan where he had played linebacker. After college when it was apparent his football career was over, he had moved to Panama City, Florida, to work as a high-school Physical Education teacher.

During his first year in Panama City, he had

met another first-year teacher who had grown up on the beautiful beaches and coastal waters of the city. Within a year, they were married, and I was born a year later. My name is Brandon Michael Barnes, but those who know me around Panama City call me Bruno. I even have close friends who never knew my real name was Brandon.

I know Bruno is not a typical nickname. In the past, I had some adults ask me if I liked the nickname. I love it! To me, Bruno was a name fit for a middle linebacker. I hoped someday my name would be mentioned with other famous linebackers like Dick Butkus, Ray Lewis, and other NFL greats.

My younger brother Max was born three years after me. His full name is Maximus Edgar Barnes, but everyone calls him Bubba. My dad loved to give kids nicknames and especially to his own two boys.

Our entire team loves our team manager, who happens to be my now eight-year-old brother Bubba. Being the football manager meant the world to

Bubba, and he took his managerial job seriously. He oversaw the organization of all the game balls, served as our water boy, and made sure my dad had everything he needed during the game.

His most important job though, and the one he valued the most, was to retrieve both teams' kicking tees. Either on the kickoff, a field goal attempt, or an extra point, Bubba would dart from the sideline and return the tee to the right team.

Bubba's job became a South Bay tradition. Both teams and fans cheered loud and long as Bubba raced around the football field in his smaller-than-usual Sharks uniform. Having my little brother serve the players on my team means the world to me. A big part of that desire was because I wanted to be like my dad. I grew up listening to all the football stories and examining every inch of Dad's old scrapbooks. They were filled with articles and pictures of my dad when he played football.

Dad used to say, "Bruno, you are a Barnes, the son of Bill Barnes. Part of your dynasty is to be a linebacker."

Linebackers, by nature, are tough, aggressive, and smart players. They are usually the biggest and hardest hitters on the team, as well as the defensive leaders.

All I have ever wanted to be is a leader. I tried to live up to that objective at every practice and in every game that I ever played. I had started at middle linebacker on every single football team I ever played on. There wasn't a single year where I didn't lead the team in tackles and sacks. I was the best middle linebacker around the Panama City area, and everyone knew it.

My two best friends, Chet Anderson and Leon Carr, were both great football players. We have played together for the past four years. Chet was our quarterback, and Leon played wide receiver and defensive back.

Our team has always been competitive and good. Last year, with most of our team being seventh graders, we went 8-1 with our only loss coming to an almost-all, eighth-grade team from Arnold Middle School.

South Bay has never had a middle school football team go undefeated.

This is going to be the year!

The first day of practice was hot and sticky, typical Florida weather in August.

I loved it.

Dad blew his whistle hard three times, signaling for all of us to meet in the middle of the football field. We quickly took a knee and focused our eyes directly on my dad.

Football is about discipline, respect, and attention to detail. Dad always talked about those three basics and made them his points of emphasis when coaching.

"I like the way we are moving today. I love the energy. Boys, it shows who put in work this summer and who is prepared. For those who didn't run and come to summer workouts, good luck," he said.

Chet, Leon, and I hadn't missed a single summer workout. We felt great being back on the football field.

The constant stream of sweat running down my face reminded me of all that I loved about football.

Dad introduced the three of us as captains to the team. He expected a lot from of us when we were on the football field and even more when we weren't. We were the team leaders; we had wanted it and had proven that we were ready.

"Everything is shaping up to make this year's football season at South Bay a magical one. I have one more little surprise that I wanted to let you know about this season," Dad said.

All the players, who were leaning on one knee, leaned in to listen more intently. My dad wasn't big on surprises or changes, so we knew his announcement must be something important.

"Our last game of the year, game 9, won't be played against Edgewater this year," Dad said.

Typically, South Bay always ended with an easy win over Edgewater. The Edgewater Dolphins had a great athletics program—in baseball and golf— but not football. They were always an easy game, and last year we won 54-0.

According to last year's football schedule, we were almost guaranteed a 9-0 season. All the players thought we would have the same schedule as the year before, *but suddenly we didn't.*

He continued, "I was able to book a game I know everyone will be excited to play in. This year our last game will be against the Seaside Mustangs."

The team tried to stifle a gasp.

Did Dad just say we were going to play the Seaside Mustangs?

-3-

The Seaside Mustangs were an elite football team. They were well known throughout the entire state of Florida for having one of the best middle-school football teams every year. In fact, they were a football powerhouse in the South, not just Florida.

Last year, *The Florida Sun,* Panama City's major newspaper, featured a front-page story in their sports section about the Mustangs. The article detailed their decade of dominance in the Western Florida panhandle. The Mustangs had twice been voted the best eighth-grade team in the entire state. This year they were loaded once again and had a quarterback named Jacoby Howard. Jacoby was the younger brother of Jackson Howard.

Last year Jackson had won the Florida Gatorade Player of the Year for the state of Florida. He had signed with the Florida Gators and was already penciled in as the starting quarterback as a true freshman. He already had NFL potential at the age of 18.

The scary thing is when Jackson signed with Florida, he made an unbelievable prediction at his press conference: "My brother Jacoby is more skilled and has a better arm than I did in middle school."

As an eighth grader, Jacoby already had offers from Florida and Florida State. Seaside had not lost a junior high football game in four years.

Even though the season hadn't started yet, I knew theirs would be the only team standing in our way from an undefeated season and a chance to write our names in the history of South Bay football.

"Bro, did your dad just say we are playing Seaside? Or am I having a strange nightmare?" asked Chet, leaning over to me so no one else on the team could hear his question.

"I think so," I said, trying not to sound surprised. At first, I was shocked. My dad hadn't mentioned anything about the game to me…and I didn't want Leon to know that.

"If we want to be the best, we have to beat the best," I whispered with conviction. I wanted to sound confident and in control—like I was happy about the game.

Deep down inside, I was *not* happy about playing the Mustangs.

All summer I had worked out with one simple goal in mind. I wanted to be the captain of the first undefeated team in South Bay history. I wanted it so bad, but I also wanted it for my dad. His love for football was something we shared, and I wanted to be the one to help deliver an undefeated season for him.

"We can beat them," I said loud enough for both Chet and Leon to hear me.

I added, "Guys, we are the captains of this team. If we are intimated by them, the rest of the team will be too."

Both nodded in agreement.

I didn't know why they were so nervous. After all, the task of stopping Jacoby Howard would be a problem for our entire defense.

I knew that.

I also knew that since I was the middle linebacker, I would be tasked with trying to slow down Howard on every play. Someone with his speed and skill set is almost impossible to stop; trying to contain him would be my main priority.

Dad's scratchy coach voice called for our attention. "Boys, forget about Seaside for now; the time to prepare for the Mustangs will come. We will focus on one day at time, one team at a time. Our first game is only a couple of weeks away—against Lynn Haven. Only Lynn Haven—no one else—is who prepare for," ended Dad.

He had always prepared us to focus weekly on our opponent. Our team would play eight games before we took the field against the Mustangs. We were scheduled to play Seaside the last game of the year on Wednesday, October 10. One of the worst things you can do in football is overlook other teams while looking ahead to other games.

How can we not think about Seaside?

I looked around the field and could feel the excitement. Images of Jacoby Howard scrambling around our football field flashed through my mind.

I knew I had to be laser focused, or we wouldn't even have a chance to be undefeated by the time Seaside came to South Bay at the end of the season. We couldn't overlook any team on our schedule.

"One game at a time...one game at a time," I kept reminding myself.

-4-

The first three weeks of the season went by fast. Our season kicked off with a 48-6 convincing win over Lynn Haven. I was so excited to finally have a football game and hit other people who weren't my teammates.

Our entire team played well. Chet threw three touchdowns with two going to Leon.

On the defensive side, I had twelve tackles and two sacks. I was in the Lynn Haven offensive back-field more than their running backs were. Near the end of third quarter, Leon intercepted a pass and ran it all the way back for a touchdown. I made a big block on our sideline to spring Leon free for the touchdown. Once he cleared the first level of players, he was gone. Leon was fast and watching him pull away from everyone as he scored a 64-yard touchdown on the interception return was amazing.

I can think of nothing I loved more than celebrating in the end zone with my team.

The next games proved to be two easy victories, and I didn't play much after halftime because we had such a commanding lead.

The Sharks were 3-0, and all three wins came in a dominating manner. A buzz was starting around Panama City. The locals knew that the Sharks were developing into a great football team.

I loved everything about growing up in Panama City. The beaches, inland waterways and excellent fishing in the Gulf of Mexico made our city a worldwide attraction for tourists. Typically, we have many year-round visitors, but most visitors come from May through the end of October.

Known as a summer town, the fall is a great time to visit my hometown. Panama City plays host to several renowned fall festivals, including the Chasin' the Sun Music Festival, the Lobster Festival, and my favorite, the Pirates of the High Seas Fest.

Each year on Columbus Day weekend, thousands of people flock to Panama City for the Pirates of the High Seas Fest. This free, family-friendly festival filled with excitement and interaction hosts scavenger hunts, a pirate invasion on the beach, a kids' parade and a huge, main attraction parade. The entire weekend offers live music and a spectacular fireworks display on Saturday night at Russell-Fields City Pier.

Our entire school, including the football team, was extra excited this year. South Bay had been chosen to be the lead float in the parade—a big honor among all the schools in Panama City. Each year, one school is honored for classroom excellence by being selected to be the first float in the parade.

Everything was coming together, and all the signs were pointing to an epic fall at South Bay.

School was crazy the week of the festival. The

local media was present all week, and our principal, Mr. McDonald, was even interviewed by a television news show out of Tallahassee.

Our football games always fell on a Wednesday, so practice was extra intense on Monday and Tuesday. The increase of attention had our players hitting harder and running faster. Our opponent, Sunnyside Middle School, wasn't going to be prepared for what was coming on Wednesday. I knew that if we practiced in this manner all the time, we would be almost unbeatable for any team—even Seaside.

By the time the first whistle blew Wednesday night, everyone was ready for a Shark feeding frenzy.

The game was over in the first eight minutes, as we took a 36-0 lead after the first quarter. Our team seemed so much faster, and we were making spectacular plays on both the offensive and defensive side of the ball.

My highlight came late in the second quarter. I

blitzed and sacked their quarterback. I hit him so hard, he fumbled the football. Without missing a beat, I scooped up the loose pigskin and rumbled 44 yards for a Shark defensive touchdown!

The game ended with a 52-14 victory, pushing our record to 4-0. After the game, all the guys were hyped and excited. I was all smiles as we took a knee at midfield for Dad's postgame speech.

"Boys, I am really, really proud of you all. This week you practiced like champions. That focus and attention to detail led to a dominant victory!" he said as the players erupted into cheers.

He smiled and let us enjoy a couple seconds of rowdiness before he raised his hand, signaling all of us to go silent.

"We are halfway there but don't lose focus. This is a fun, crazy weekend with the festival. I expect you to act and demonstrate the kind of character that makes the Sharks so special," Dad said.

He added, "Don't forget, Mr. McDonald has asked the football team to lead the South Bay Shark float this year. What an honor! Make sure you show up in your uniform at 10:30 a.m. on Saturday to line up for the parade."

I beamed with excitement. For the first time, South Bay would be leading the parade. The whole city of Panama would be seeing Shark football players in the front, where we finally belonged.

Saturday finally arrived as Bubba and I raced to our school's float. We passed many other schools along the parade line. With each one, my heart swelled that they were watching us in our Shark uniforms heading to the front of the line.

When we finally made it to the front, my heart dropped.

South Bay still had the lead float, but I couldn't believe who they placed right behind us as the second float.

-5-

The Seaside Mustangs were the second float!

Of all the schools in Panama City? There has to be over 30 other schools in the parade line. Why in the world would the organizers put Seaside behind us? I thought.

The green-and-white school colors of the Mustangs were everywhere.

"Dude," mentioned Leon, "I just saw Jacoby Howard."

"So?" I responded sharply.

"I am just saying…I was thinking about asking him for an autograph," Leon said.

I turned and shot Leon a look.

"I don't think so. Come on, man. We have to

prepare to beat them. The last thing you should be thinking about is asking him for an autograph. That's embarrassing," I said sternly.

"Dude, it's one football game," Chet said softly. Chet was always quieter, which meant his words always held a lot of weight with me.

"I know, but it's going to be the type of game everyone will remember; this is our chance," I said.

"It's one game," Chet said again.

Beating Seaside had become an obsession for me. I was starting to realize I was so consumed with wanting to win that game that I was missing out on many of the great things our football team was doing. I really wanted to enjoy everything, but I just couldn't get my mind off the Mustangs.

I knew Chet was right but being right and being okay with it are two different matters.

Other Shark teammates were starting to show up for the parade. Everyone had a good laugh when Louie, our starting center, showed up with the wrong color jersey. He was the only one standing in his white jersey among a sea of blue jerseys.

Dad had told us at least three times at the end of Friday's practice to wear our blue uniforms.

"Nice one, Louie," I commented as he ran up.

"My fault, I forgot. It's fine," he said.

"Okay, you definitely will stand out in the parade," I said with a grin. Louie usually stood out no matter where we went.

Our float looked great. The South Bay Student Council had designed a huge great white shark outfitted with a pirate hat and an eye patch. The shark was eating a huge treasure chest filled with pirate gold.

About 100 students, including 35 football players, were there. I looked at the crowd and made eye contact with my dad. He was smiling from ear to ear. I could tell he was proud of his team, proud of his two sons, and proud to be a Shark.

The loudspeaker on the street clicked on, crackling as the broadcaster announced, "The parade will be starting in two minutes." After the announcement, I started hearing a strange buzz coming from behind us.

As minutes passed, the noise grew louder and louder, even getting everyone's attention at our float. I turned to see what all the noise was about.

Standing directly behind us, was a mob of Seaside football players. Their green jerseys reflected brightly behind us.

Jacoby Howard, who was out in front of everyone else, stood staring and laughing. His fresh fade haircut and jewelry sparkled in the sun. He took the role of a superstar to the next level. His gold chain was adorned with a big, heavy gold #13 on it.

Well before seeing his number, I recognized who he was. If I didn't know better, I would have thought he was at least a sophomore.

Our eyes met. "Hey, Buddy, you better help your boy next time," he said sarcastically.

"*Buddy?* Did he just call me *Buddy*?" I asked myself.

"My name is Bruno, and I am no buddy of yours," I shot back. In my mind, I heard my dad's words of wisdom after practice reminding us to be quiet and not to respond. I ignored his instruction.

The entire crowd became quiet and tense as kids from both schools waited to see who would make the next move.

"Just wait until we clobber you! You won't have so much to say then!" a voice from behind me boomed loudly.

"Who in his right mind would say that?" I asked myself, turning around.

It was Bubba, and he was pointing directly at Jacoby!

-6-

An awkward hush fell over the crowd. Bubba was always one to speak his mind, but even he had to know that he was pointing at Jacoby Howard.

Jacoby looked around shocked. He knew he had to respond and was searching for exactly what to say next. Finally, after a short pause, he responded, "Little man, I like your attitude. But do you know just who you are talking to?"

"Yeah, I know who you are. You know what else? I know my brother is going to stomp you when you play the South Bay Sharks! I know that too," bragged Bubba.

My heart sank as the crowd of kids from South Bay began cheering loudly. *What is my brother doing? Is he trying to destroy any chance we have of beating the Mustangs?*

"Is that so?" asked Jacoby.

"It is," he said proudly.

"Listen, Jacoby. He doesn't mean anything or know what he is saying. He's my little brother, our team manager; he's young," I said, trying to diffuse the situation.

Jacoby stared me down.

Shaking his head, he said, "You might want to teach him some manners. But don't worry; if you don't, I will teach all of you South Bay boys some real soon!"

"Is that so?" I asked.

"Yeah, that's right. So far, nobody has stopped Jacoby Howard," he said.

"Well, good thing! We aren't a bunch of nobodies. We are the Sharks!" I replied.

Suddenly, I felt a firm hand on my shoulder.

I turned to see Mr. McDonald, and his timing was perfect. The crowd of kids settled back and crept back to their floats.

"Boys…all good?" Mr. McDonald asked.

"All good, sir. My buddy and me were just talking football, that's all," Jacoby said.

He called me "Buddy" again…

On the inside I was steaming, but I didn't want Mr. McDonald to know.

"All good, sir. Let's celebrate South Bay's leading this parade," I said with a smile.

By then a couple more staff members had caught wind of the conversation and had appeared. Things were calming down as I turned back toward the front of the float.

I walked over and grabbed Bubba by the arm.

"What in the world were you thinking?" I asked him bluntly.

He shrugged his shoulders and gave me a small smirk. He wasn't the one who would have to tackle Jacoby during the game. That last thing I wanted to do was make one of the best eighth-grade football players in Florida angry.

In my heart, I knew I couldn't be too upset at Bubba. He was a proud little brother who thought he was sticking up for his big brother and the football team.

I rubbed the top of Bubba's head and said, "Little bro, next time save the talking to me," I said with a smile.

He knew that a small part of me was proud of him for sticking up for me.

Little did I know our little run-in with Jacoby and the Mustangs was only the beginning of a massive storm that was yet to come.

-7-

The streets were lined with people celebrating the Pirates of the High Seas Fest. In the bay, a giant pirate ship was floating around blasting other ships with water guns and a huge water cannon.

The atmosphere was awesome and festive. The parade lasted about 20 minutes before concluding at Pier Park, adjacent to Russell-Fields Pier.

"Hey, Bruno, let's go check out Ron Jon Surf Shop," said Chet. We always liked to hang out and shop in the cool stores at Pier Park. With over 124 stores to shop in and tons of great places to eat, we had plenty of places to visit.

"Can I go with you guys?" asked Bubba.

"No way," I said. I loved Bubba, and we got along

great, but in no way did a 14 year old want to have his 8-year-old brother following him around.

"Come on, man! It's cool. We love Bubba," Chet said.

"Oh, all right, fine," I said reluctantly.

Bubba, Chet, Leon, and I took off to spend the next couple of hours shopping at Pier Place. After browsing in the various shops, we decided to grab a pizza from Great White Pizza. The four of sat down and gobbled up one of their signature pizzas, the Bruce Special.

This meat-themed specialty pizza was loaded with mozzarella, beef, pepperoni, Canadian bacon, sausage, and bacon. After we had devoured our handmade pizza and stepped outside, we noticed it was getting closer and closer to dusk.

We had plans to meet our parents next door at Russell-Fields Pier to watch the extravaganza. One of the crown jewels of the Pirates of the High Seas festival was the Saturday night fireworks.

We had about ten minutes before the fireworks started as we headed out of Pier Park.

"Can we please stop and get some Dippin' Dots on our way out?" Bubba asked.

I had no idea how he could still be hungry.

"Yeah, the stand is by the exit, but we told Mom and Dad we would be there by 7:55 p.m. I don't want to be late, and I don't want to miss any of the fireworks," I said.

We said goodbye to Chet and Leon, and they headed toward a different exit so Bubba could get his favorite ice cream treat—Cookie Dough Dippin' Dots. I told him to order the largest size and even paid for them. His face lit up as he started to shovel the Dippin' Dots into his mouth. As we turned the corner toward the exit, I could see Russell-Fields Pier in the background. We had to hustle to make the time our parents had expected us.

A loud boom that sounded like a pirate's cannon rocked our ears. *The fireworks at the Pirates of the High Seas Fest is starting earlier than everyone planned!*

"We got to go now, Bubba! That is the sign the

fireworks are about to start," I said as we both started to weave through crowds of people who were still shopping at Pier Park. I grabbed Bubba's hand as we picked up the pace and maneuvered through the mob of people.

Suddenly, I realized my hand was empty. Panicked I spun around, but I didn't see Bubba anywhere. I started running back toward the Dippin' Dots stand, calling his name.

After running 20 yards or so, I found him surrounded by Mustang football players. He was sitting on the ground surrounded by a pile of spilled Dippin' Dots.

- 8 -

I ran up and pushed the first Mustang jersey that was closest to my brother.

"Whoa! Easy, man!" came a voice from the pack of green jerseys.

I spun to see Jacoby.

"Bruno..." Bubba tried to talk, but I wasn't hearing none of it.

"You got a problem?" I said glaring face to face into Jacoby's eyes.

"Bruno..." Bubba said again louder.

"You are going to have a big problem if you don't chill," Jacoby said.

I reached down to pick up Bubba, wiping off his shorts and shirt.

The rage inside of me was real, and I was about to explode. In my mind, I already knew what had happened. *These Mustangs wanted to get back at my little brother for his lipping off to Jacoby earlier at the parade. I don't need to be a genius to figure that out.*

Once I got him up, I put Bubba behind me.

"Who's the funny guy? Who thinks he is tough for tripping an eight-year-old kid?" I yelled.

"Bruno, I think it was an accident," Bubba said sheepishly from behind me.

I turned and looked at Bubba then back to the group of about six or seven Mustangs.

"Yeah, it was just an accident," said one of the other Mustang players.

"Pretty convenient accident, don't you think?" I retorted.

For a couple of seconds, there was silence.

"Buddy, I don't know what you think happened, but the facts are facts. Your brother tripped on his own. We didn't trip him," said Jacoby.

"Bruno...Bruno, I think I tripped on the cement," said Bubba. I glanced down and spotted several cracks in the cement that could have caused him to trip.

"I know how this looks, but we don't go around tripping little kids," said Jacoby.

"Even the ones who mouth off to you?" I asked.

"Yes, even the ones who mouth off to us," he said confidently.

My mind was racing, and I was starting to think that maybe I had overreacted. *Chances are they're telling the truth.*

"I have half of my cup left. It's okay, Bruno. Let's go; Mom and Dad are waiting for us," said Bubba.

I nodded and started to take big steps backward, slowly stepping away from the Mustangs. I made sure to keep my eyes on the swarm of football players.

"Next time you better make sure you know what you're talking about before you talk to us like that," snickered one of the bigger football players.

I could tell the situation wasn't over, and I had really angered them by accusing them of tripping

Bubba. I was still trying to control my initial anger as well.

The big player and another Mustang stepped out of the group toward me. They were acting aggressive. *It's a six-on-one situation.* I knew this situation was dangerous for Bubba and me. I really wished Chet and Leon were still with us. Even with those two, the odds were still bad for us.

I backed up as the two bruisers approached me.

"If this happens, you run," I whispered to Bubba.

Just as the two boys stood an arm's length from us, Jacoby stepped in. "Chill out! This isn't happening—not like this," he said.

The boys looked annoyed at first and then realizing Jacoby was the one interfering, they quickly backed up.

"That's his little brother," he said, staring at both. With that strong statement, the Mustang players turned and walked back into Pier Park.

-9-

"Don't open your mouth about this to Mom and Dad," I warned Bubba as we jogged to the pier to meet them.

"I won't. Do you think we could go back so I can get Jacoby Howard's autograph?" he quickly asked.

I could tell he was proud of his big brother for defending him—even if we were outnumbered. I decided to ignore his autograph comment and not respond. My blood boiled when I thought of Jacoby Howard. Everyone thought he was the greatest—even my little brother. I was getting so sick of hearing people talk about him.

"You didn't look scared," said Bubba.

"That's good because I was. You know I wouldn't

let anything happen to you—even if you do annoy me," I said laughing.

We arrived at the Russell-Fields Pier just as the first of the fireworks exploded overhead. The explosion painted the dark sky with a rainbow of vibrant colors. The pier was packed, and it seemed like everyone was wearing some type of pirate gear. Dad even had this cheap plastic hook over his right hand.

"Dad, really," I said motioning to the hook.

"Arguuh, matey! Had me hand taken off by a great white shark," he said in his cheesiest pirate voice. I loved the pirate gear and theme but didn't have much patience for Dad's pirate voice or hook. Our family sat and enjoyed the fireworks show before heading back toward Pier Park to our car.

The fireworks display was magnificent. With all the festival excitement, I was overly tired after a long day. The festival was great fun, but I was getting tired of seeing the Mustangs around. We hadn't even played yet, and a part of me wanted to see them lose before our game. The pressure on both teams being undefeated would make the game stakes high.

Everyone around Panama City knew that we were the only team that could even begin to compete with Seaside. But not a person outside of our football team thought we could keep the score within 20 points against the Mustangs.

Dad always told me that it didn't matter what other people thought. It only mattered what every coach and player in our locker room thought.

I knew that most of our players were scared to death of Seaside and Jacoby Howard. I was too, but I planned on using whatever fear I had as motivation to win.

The two incidents with the Mustangs today made me want to win even more. A Shark victory would be that much sweeter against those cocky players from Seaside.

Would the game still be as interesting if both teams weren't undefeated? I wondered. I could think of several one-loss teams at South Bay, but never an undefeated team.

I knew I had to bring my attention back to our next opponent, or we could lose a game we should win. I had to convince myself not to worry about Seaside. *Who was the most important team we were playing? The next one on our schedule.*

Every day I kept telling myself that. At practice, I tried to be a good leader and prepare the team for our next opponent.

In the back of my mind, however, I couldn't shake off Jacoby and the rest of the Mustangs. I noticed the same focus in other players too.

Our next game we won a sloppy game 26-18 against Callaway, a team we should have beaten by 40 points. As sharp and as focused as we had been in the first three games, we looked the opposite against Callaway. Even though we had way more talent, it didn't show against these opponents. Everything we did looked slow and out of sync. If it hadn't been for a late kickoff return by Leon, we might have lost the football game.

After the game, Dad said what we were already feeling.

"Boys, we have talked and talked about this. We are not playing Seaside until week 9! We still have three more opponents before Seaside; that is our focus," he screamed.

He added, "Football is so much like life. Each week you must prepare every day for what is directly in front of you. That is all you can control. I promise you, there will be a time when we devote everything we got to Seaside."

We had to win the next three games before we would get our shot at the Mustangs.

Four weeks?

I didn't know if my mind could handle four more weeks of Jacoby Howard's dancing through it.

-10-

Over the next two weeks, our football team dug in and focused. Every day we worked hard and concentrated primarily on our opponent. Seaside was always in the back of our minds, but I knew we would be in good shape if we kept them back there.

With laser-like focus, we demolished both teams on our way to easy wins, pushing us to 6-0 on the season.

I read the sports section in the *Panama City Sun* every Saturday morning, keeping track of Seaside. The Mustangs continued to blow out their opponents. Their offense was putting up record numbers. Not one team thus far had been able to hold the Mustangs under 50 points. In fact, they were averaging 55 points per contest.

Not a good sign for any defense.

Week seven was a huge week for us; we faced North Bay Haven on the schedule.

Seaside had to play Sunnyside, a team we had already beaten 52-14 earlier in the season.

North Bay Haven would be our toughest opponent to face so far. They were well coached and fast. Their head coach was a former college football player. Coach McLaughlin, or Coach Mac as he was called, was highly respected, and his teams were always prepared and played hard.

Coach Mac would spend time scouting our team. He would look for weaknesses and tendencies that he could use against us in the football game.

Dad and Coach Mac had become friends over the years of coaching against each other. They often attended football conferences together and talked over game plans. During the week of the game against each other, the two coaches did not speak to each other—out of respect—not because of competitiveness.

The two men had an immense respect for each other. Dad knew the game with Bay Haven would be a good indicator of exactly how prepared our football team was. The annual game versus Bay Haven was an October tradition in Panama City.

Even though it was now early October, the weather had remained unseasonably hot—even by Florida standards.

When practice started on Monday, I could tell several of our players were distracted and lacked focus. Their distraction came to the forefront when we quit scrimmaging to take our first water break. As I walked toward the water bottles, I overheard some seventh graders talking.

"I have never seen anything like him. He's too fast," one said.

"No one in Florida can stop him. He's not even human," another said.

I simply listened, knowing they had to be talking about Jacoby, acting like I was getting more water as they kept talking. The way they were bragging about Jacoby's abilities, you would have thought he had already won the Heisman trophy.

After hearing all I could handle, I cleared my throat loud enough to cause the group of boys to turn around. Once they saw it was me, they lowered their heads and walked away.

Chet jogged up as I was finishing my water break.

"Did you see it?" he asked.

"See what?" I replied.

Chet took an awkward glance toward Leon.

"See what?" I repeated.

"The clip from last weekend's game," said Leon.

Still lost, I simply stared at both of them. They could tell I had no idea what they were talking about.

"I'll show you after practice," Chet said.

Dad's whistle blasted, signaling that practice was resuming.

What clip? What had Jacoby done so well that all the players were talking about it?

I already knew what a dynamite player he was. Every weekend social media was filled with clips and people bragging about Jacoby Howard.

So what could he have done that was so amazing that Chet had to show me the video?

Whatever it was, it had to be spectacular; Chet didn't get excited about too much. He has never been a big fan of Jacoby but knew his athletic ability was off the charts.

"Man, this must be something if Chet is talking about it," I said to myself.

The rest of practice I was off; in fact, I was lousy. I went in the wrong direction and bungled several defensive calls. When we went live action, offensive versus defensive, I dropped an easy interception.

I had lost focus; my mind was on Jacoby.

"Focus, focus and effort, Bruno! Let's go," Dad bellowed. Obviously, I was not myself, but I couldn't shake everyone's admiration for Jacoby.

I had one of the worst practices of my life. I had let Jacoby run wild, and we hadn't even played yet.

I was losing the mental game of football.

After practice, Dad gave me the look—the one that says, "Okay, it's time to get it together now."

I was going to change my thoughts and refocus on North Bay Haven...at least that is what I thought...

That whole intention changed when I saw the clip Chet was talking about.

-11-

Watching football clips and short videos on our cell phones was nothing new. Every day during lunch, we would watch various football players in action or amazing videos.

The clips ranged from high-school players to professionals, but every week Jacoby had done something in his game clip worthy. Some videos had him out running defenses, juking two or three defenders, and throwing bombs to his receivers. All his video clips were impressive, especially for an eighth grader.

But none compared to this new one...

After practice, I rushed to change and meet Chet. Both Chet and Leon were waiting for me.

Chet motioned me over, holding out his cell phone. He turned and showed me the face of the phone. I nodded, and he knew to begin.

The clip started with Jacoby back in the shotgun. He was wearing the same green uniform he had on at Pier Park. He clapped his hands, and the center snapped the ball back to him.

Jacoby took the ball and dropped to pass. The other team blitzed, sending in both of their linebackers to stop Jacoby.

Effortlessly, Jacoby stepped right and then left. He did it so fast, the move took both defenders by surprise. Watching the clip was almost like seeing everyone but Jacoby moving in slow motion.

With his fast juke move, the two defenders ran right into each other as Jacoby danced past them.

I turned and looked at them.

"Wow! That is pretty crazy! I don't know if I have ever seen anyone move like that," I admitted.

Chet turned and looked at me. "Keep watching, Bruno; you haven't seen anything yet."

I watched as Jacoby made several other moves

causing defenders to miss and tackle air as he accelerated down the field toward the end zone. First, he went ten yards, then twenty as he crisscrossed around the field.

It was the most spectacular football play I had ever seen.

Chet could tell I was impressed.

"Just keep watching," he said again.

The best play was yet to come. The safety was the only one standing between Jacoby and a remarkable touchdown run.

The safety was in front and looked to be squared up in perfect position to tackle Jacoby.

I find it incredibly hard to explain what happened next.

I watched as the safety came flying toward Jacoby only to have the quarterback leap high to hurdle him. Jacoby's perfectly timed jump cleared the top of the defender, and his feet hit the ground in perfect unison.

Howard ran the last ten yards for a Seaside touchdown.

His run was truly the greatest play I had ever seen—ever.

I didn't know what to think or feel on the way home.

That video of his run was everywhere on social media.

When I got home, I heard the sports announcer on the news talking about an unbelievable play at a football game. I ran out to see the same clip playing on our family television.

Jacoby Howard was now going viral; in an instant he was a television star.

Negative thoughts went through my mind.

Was I just going to be another part of one of his highlight reels?

Was he going to embarrass South Bay?

Did Jacoby Howard plan to make me just another of his victims?

-12-

"What's wrong, son?" Dad asked as I sat staring at my plate of spaghetti.

Dinnertime has always been important to our family. A priority of ours has been to sit down and eat a meal together every night. My parents have always emphasized the power of family and faith. So, every night, no matter what time, we have always gathered as a family, prayed together, and enjoyed the meal together.

"Nothing—just a lot on my mind," I said, curling the noodles on my fork.

Dad continued to stare at me.

He knows me too well.

"Dad, he is scared Jacoby Howard is going to

make him look like a fool, and the whole world will see it," piped up Bubba.

I had showed Bubba the clips after practice. My younger brother said nothing and just stared with his mouth wide open at the highlight.

"Whatever…I am not scared," I quickly shot back, glaring at Bubba as he scarfed down dinner. Without even looking up, he replied, "Yes, you are! And I would be too!"

"Bruno, are you?" Dad asked.

"Am I what?" I asked.

"Are you scared to play Seaside? Jacoby Howard?" Dad asked.

"No, I mean…I just want to win so bad. South Bay has to go undefeated this year," I dodged his question.

"Are you scared?" Dad repeated firmly.

I was starting to get irritated with Dad's constant prodding about Jacoby.

"Son, it's okay to be afraid," Dad said.

When he said those words, my body instantly relaxed. Hearing him say that was like sweet music to my ears. The truth of it was, I was afraid. I was afraid to miss tackles, get embarrassed, and lose the game. As I thought about it, I was mostly afraid of losing to Seaside. I didn't want miss tackles and be embarrassed. The last thing I wanted to do was cause our team to lose.

"Listen, Bruno, life is about doing the right things and having a winning mentality. That means you give your best effort, and whatever the outcome is, you are a winner," Dad explained.

He quickly added, "We are having a great season. You are a fantastic football player and a pure joy to me as my son. That alone makes me so proud. One football game could never change that."

I felt good hearing my dad say that. Deep down, I knew he felt that way. He preached at practice the importance of hard work and best effort; he never, ever spoke about winning and losing.

Dad was such a good role model and coach, I wanted to win the Seaside game for him too.

But if we lost, would that change anything?
No, it wouldn't.

Our season would be legendary simply because of the morals and life lessons we had learned that year. Going undefeated or 8-1 wouldn't change any of that.

I was so glad that we talked about it at the dinner table. This entire football season hadn't been my most enjoyable.

I realized I had become too worried and wrapped up about going undefeated. Instead, I needed to enjoy each game—win or lose.

Winning truly was in the effort and focus of the game. The scoreboard was usually just a reward for those who did the things needed to win. Sometimes no matter how well a team played, the other team possessed more talent. You could still do your absolute best and come out on the losing side. But that didn't make any players losers.

I got up and cleaned off my dish before putting it in the sink. I felt like a huge weight had been lifted off my shoulders. And that was the moment that Jacoby Howard stopped running through my mind.

I still planned on doing everything in my power to stop him and to help our team beat Seaside. I also knew that no matter what, this was a season I would remember for the rest of my life.

Little did I know what was about to happen. This season would be one that no one in the state of Florida would ever forget.

The storm brewing inside my mind was nothing compared to the one over the Gulf of Mexico.

-13-

North Bay Haven was good—extremely good.

Coach Mac had his team ready. Clearly, he had watched many of our game tapes. He already knew our play on every snap of the ball. When Leon lined up wide, Coach Mac audibled his defense and countered our offensive play. When we brought Leon into the backfield, he knew we were running a sweep to the strong side of the field.

This was the first time I had ever played against a coach who rivaled my dad in gamesmanship and football knowledge. It seemed like no matter what we did, they were ready for it.

The first half went back and forth. Bay Haven had the ball on the 30-yard line with 5 seconds to go in the first half. We were tied at 14-14 and needed to keep them out of the end zone to go into halftime tied.

"We need to keep them out; no matter what, they can't get behind anyone. If they gain a couple yards, it's not a big deal. This will be the last play of the half, and they have to score," Dad said.

North Bay Haven lined up in a spread formation with one running back lined up next to the quarterback. I knew that one back was mine. Everyone was locked in with one of their wide receivers. *Wherever that running back goes, I'll be there.*

The quarterback surveyed our defense and yelled out an audible, adjusting to something he saw. I stood locked into the running back.

As the quarterback snapped the ball, the running back jogged to the right. I shuffled and kept the running back in full vision, knowing he was not much of a threat to score a touchdown. The quarterback scrambled, causing me to come up from my linebacker position. As he turned to throw, I was already flying toward the running back.

The ball was a perfect short toss to his man. I zoomed toward the running back, knowing time had expired ending the first half. Out of the corner of my eye, I saw Leon flying up toward the running back as well.

Right before the two of us tackled him, the running back stopped.

I knew what was happening but didn't have time to stop it. He reared back his arm and threw a long pass to one of his wide receivers who was standing wide open for a touchdown. Leon had left him to come up and tackle the running back.

North Bay Haven had orchestrated a perfect halfback pass, catching our entire defense off guard. After kicking the extra point, we went into the locker room trailing 21-14. For the first time all season, we were behind at halftime. The trick play had shifted all the momentum in favor of North Bay Haven. I could feel all the energy and enthusiasm sucked out of the room as I entered the locker room.

I was mad—more at myself than Leon.

I should have known better, and being the leader, I should have prepared our defense better. In the heat of the moment, North Bay Haven had used our aggressiveness against us.

"Lesson learned," I told myself.

Dad was calm and pointed out how well both teams were playing. He gave a lot of credit to North Bay Haven, telling us that the game was ours if we wanted it.

"Forget about the last play. If they have to resort to using trick plays to score, we are in good shape. Defense will win this game for us in the second half," Dad said.

The Shark players roared as we sprinted out of the visitors' locker room toward the football field.

"That is the last time they will see the end zone," I told myself.

I knew after this half, win or lose, we could finally start talking and planning for Seaside.

We needed to own this half of the game.

-14-

We came out more focused and shut down North Bay Haven's first drive, giving the ball back to the offense. On a third and five, Chet found Leon streaking wide open down the sideline for a 63-yard touchdown pass. Neal, our kicker, tied the game on the extra-point kick.

Both teams fought hard and went back and forth late into the fourth quarter. With the defense of both teams playing well, neither gave much away to either offense.

I glanced up at the clock to see 2:00 minutes remaining in the game. We had the ball on the North Bay Haven 30-yard line.

I knew something crazy had to happen for us to

go the 70 yards for a game-winning touchdown. It was third down.

Dad called a time out. "If we don't get this, we have to punt and force them to go the length of the field to win," Dad said.

All the players nodded.

"How long is overtime?" I asked.

Dad took a deep breath. "There is no over-time...either you win, lose, or tie," Dad said.

Tie? Even though we would still be considered undefeated with a tie, I knew it wouldn't be the same as a win. *We have to be undefeated when we play Seaside,* I thought.

I looked around the huddle and could see dis-appointment in the eyes of my teammates. Before we broke the huddle, I said, "We aren't tying this game; we are winning this game!"

North Bay Haven stopped us on third down, and Dad sent the punting team out on the field. Disappointed, our offense jogged off the field with their heads down.

I called the defense on the sideline over as our

punter boomed a great 40-yard punt. North Bay Haven caught the ball, and their returner was forced out of bounds after a short two-yard gain.

"It's up to us. Our defense will win this game. Look at me! All of you, look into my eyes. We are going to win this game," I yelled.

On first down, North Bay Haven ran off tackle for two yards and used their last time out. With 1:38 left on the clock, both teams were now out of time outs. North Bay Haven was on our 40-yard line and needed 60 yards for the game-winning touchdown.

In no way am I going to let that happen!

Without any time outs, North Bay Haven came out in a spread formation with no running backs. They had to pass to move the ball. Their only hope was to get big chunks of yards passing, pick up a first down, or get out of bounds to stop the clock.

There was no way they were getting into the end zone.

I have a plan.

-15-

North Bay Haven threw underneath to their wide receivers, eating up the clock. We were in a special defense that took away the deep ball. As long as we kept them in front of us, we knew they weren't going to score.

Their team not scoring wasn't going to be enough; we had to win.

The red numbers on the clock read 8 seconds, and North Bay Haven had the ball on the 52-yard line.

"It's now or never," I told myself.

On the last play, North Bay Haven's wide receiver had stepped out of bounds, stopping the clock and setting up one last play.

Everyone knew a Hail Mary pass was their only hope.

In the huddle, I grabbed Leon.

"Listen up! Here's what I want you to do. I am going to blitz, and the football is going to come loose. Pick up that pigskin and do the rest," I said.

Leon looked at me, nodding. He knew they had to score so he planned on dropping deep into coverage to stop a last-second touchdown.

"Trust me," I said, "set in the flats and be ready." Leon had been my friend and teammate long enough to know when I was serious about something. We broke the huddle and lined up.

North Bay Haven came out with five wide receivers and no running backs. I knew they would do this, and the play would also leave their quarterback unprotected.

The quarterback surveyed the field as I sat in the middle directly eye to eye with the signal caller. I wanted him to see me positioned in the middle.

Right before he snapped the ball, I ran to my right, just outside the defensive end.

I timed the snap of the ball perfectly and angled directly to the quarterback who naturally rolled to the right, his throwing arm side. The adrenaline was coursing through my veins, and I ran as fast I ever had. Just as the quarterback dropped back and planted on his back foot, I hit him.

As I hit him, I swiped down with my arms, stripping the football loose. The force of the hit pushed the football out a couple of yards away from the collision. I tumbled to the ground with the quarterback in my arms. We landed with a loud thud. I quickly rolled and went to my knees just in time to see Leon scoop up the football. Leon raced down the middle of the field alone as the clock expired. His speed was unmatched on the football field, and I knew no one on North Bay Haven's roster could catch him from behind.

The referee threw up his arms, signaling for a touchdown as our crowd went crazy. Players were running around hugging each other on the field. What a miraculous way to end the game! I was super excited but surprisingly calm.

I felt a huge sense of relief when I saw Leon pass the goal line. I wanted to beat North Bay Haven, but in my mind, I was even happier for a different reason.

Now, we could finally plan and talk about Seaside. Both teams were undefeated. Now I could face the storm that was brewing in my mind for Jacoby and the Mustangs.

Little did I know the storm hadn't even started yet…

-16-

The week of the Seaside game was finally here. The build up around the game was huge. The *Panama City Sun* ran a huge front-page article about the game, featuring large, full-color pictures of Jacoby and me.

I blushed when Dad held up the paper Monday morning to show it to me.

I thought being featured was a nice honor, but personally I didn't do well in the spotlight. I liked to work from the shadows and wasn't comfortable when people complimented me. By the time I got to school that morning, everyone had seen the article. Several of the guys on my team called me "Hollywood" and said, "You're famous now!"

I didn't pay much attention to the noise.

I could not wait to prep for Seaside.

The game was scheduled for Wednesday night, so we had two days left to prepare to stop Jacoby and the rest of the Mustangs. Dad and I had watched highlight footage and game tapes of the Mustangs the entire weekend.

It isn't looking good...

There were very few weaknesses to note, and Jacoby was everything everyone said he was. Very seldom are players hyped as much as he was, but he was the one who could do it all.

Practice became so intense that Dad had to stop us. "Listen, guys, I get this is a big game. But if we keep hitting like this, we won't have enough guys left to play on Wednesday," he said with a smirk.

Guys were flying around, especially on the defensive side. Shoulder pads were popping! The Sharks were going to give the Mustangs everything they had.

Dad had come up with an excellent game plan. I knew it would give us the best chance to win.

Our plan was to always keep me in the middle of the field keying on the football. Leon was going to come as another linebacker. His only job was to shadow and follow Jacoby wherever he went. We would miss Leon's speed on the outside but knew if Jacoby turned the corner, he would be gone anyway.

To have a chance to win, we had to contain Jacoby and keep him inside between the tackles. All his runs had to be to the inside of the field; we couldn't let him break any outside runs.

Practice was long, and we worked hard. Dad's whistle blew, I took a knee, sweaty and exhausted. Our Monday practice was excellent.

"Boys, great day, great day! One more practice tomorrow then it's game time. Get a good night's sleep tonight and be ready to go back to work tomorrow," Dad said.

He added, "You should all be proud of yourselves. This is the first time in our history that a junior-high game has sold out. Mr. McDonald said over 2,000 tickets were sold!"

Over 2,000 tickets selling for a junior-high football game? Unbelievable!

Media would be in attendance as well. The rumor was Channel 2 News planned on broadcasting live from the game!

The pressure to win just got amped up. All eyes would be on me and the rest of my Shark teammates.

Can we beat the Mustangs?

Will we be the team to give them their first loss in four years?

Can we stop Jacoby Howard?

-17-

The next morning, I sat eating cereal at our kitchen table, waiting for Bubba to finish getting ready. Mom was planning to drop us off at school.

This was our team's last practice and the day before the biggest game of my life.

As I ate, I noticed my parents were sitting in the living room, glued to the morning news. Both had a serious look of concern on their face. I got up, emptied my bowl in the trash, then walked over to the sink, dropping off my bowl. As I walked into the living room, I could tell something wasn't quite right.

"This could be a big one, folks. Everyone along the Florida Panhandle should be watching this storm with serious concern," reported a middle-aged news anchor on Channel 2.

"Dad, what is he talking about?" I asked.

Dad didn't even turn to look at me. He was so captivated by the broadcast he didn't even realize I was standing there.

"Looks like a storm is brewing out in the Gulf. It could be a big one," Mom answered.

A storm?

We had been through plenty of storms living in Panama City. The Gulf of Mexico had an uneven temper when it comes to the weather.

Storms were nothing new.

"We are monitoring a large tropical storm just west of Cuba," reported the weatherman.

"Dad, it's far away. What are the chances it actually hits Panama City?" I asked.

"I don't know, Bruno, but it doesn't look good," Dad said.

Mom elbowed Dad's ribs, bringing his gaze away from the television set.

"Son, a storm is nothing we can control anyway.

But practice today is something that is totally in our control. We need to bring the energy tonight," said Dad.

"I will," I said confidently.

When we arrived at school, there was a strange buzz about the storm. Around every corner the school kids seemingly were whispering and talking about the potential storm. I heard some people mention details like huge waves and lightning. A couple of kids even mentioned the word *hurricane*.

When I heard that word, I froze. I had seen a small hurricane when I was younger, and the strength of the storm was frightening. I was starting to get more and more nervous about the coming storm.

I walked on toward the eighth-grade hallway.

"How do so many people already know about it? With it so far away, why are people making such a big deal about it?" I asked myself.

I knew Chet and Leon would have no idea about the storm. They only looked at the television to play video games or to watch sports.

I walked up to them as they were opening their locker for first hour.

"What's up?" I asked them.

"Man, you hear about this storm down by Cuba?" Leon asked.

"Not you guys too," I groaned.

"Looks bad, man—really bad," Chet said.

"Guys, we can't control the weather. Talking about a storm that might not even hit us is the last thing we need today. Don't you even remember we play Seaside tomorrow?! Besides I heard the weatherman say it was *a tropical storm,* and we have seen plenty of those."

I made up my mind not to talk about the storm with anyone. If someone brought it up, I just played it off like it wasn't a big deal.

I was focused on practice. I felt a ton of relief when the 3:00 p.m. bell dismissed school.

It was time for football practice, my favorite part of my day.

I had no idea what was going on in the middle of the Gulf of Mexico. While we practiced on the football field, the tropical storm was morphing into a monster.

The National Weather Center then issued a dire warning, changing the status of the tropical storm to a hurricane.

My focus, though, was solely on the Seaside Mustangs and stopping Jacoby Howard.

We would finally have our chance to see if we could become South Bay legends.

-18-

When people mention the calm before the storm, they are referring to a quiet period before something intense or trouble hits. We were in the calm; there was no sign of danger. The weather was beautiful, with no sign of chaos or destruction.

When I thought about what the calm before the storm meant, it reminded me of the game of football. Everything is calm before the whistle blows, then it's on.

Game day was finally here, and it was the kind of day that led many to the gorgeous beaches of Panama City. Our town is flocked with travelers flying in from all over the world to escape the unpredictable fall weather. My dad often commented on what the weather was like in his home state of Michigan. At times it snowed in October in Michigan!

But not here! Panama City was in the mid-70s and sunny. The sun hung high and bright; the blue sky was pure without a sign of a cloud anywhere.

Walking into the school at South Bay, the electricity was flowing throughout the school. Everyone had stopped talking about the storm and talked football. The entire school was decked out in Shark clothing, and signs filled the hallways.

Our guys were walking around confident, but not cocky. There was a big difference in knowing you could win and being cocky. We knew we had a chance to beat the Mustangs.

I felt even better when I saw Chet and Leon. Both were calm and focused. We talked about our math test that was coming up during fifth hour. We talked briefly about the game.

We were focused and as ready as we could be for Seaside.

At the end of school, we had a huge pep assembly in the gym. Dad fired up the crowd as the entire student body chanted "Sharks, Sharks!" Having our entire school behind us was great, and the team was mentally and physically ready for the game.

Each player was called out and after introductions, Dad handed me the microphone.

I wasn't prepared, but I felt a sense of urgency as the rowdy crowd went silent. I said the first thing that came into my mind—the *only* thought that came to my mind: "If you miss the game tonight, you will regret it for the rest of your life."

The students went crazy!

The stage was set for the biggest game in the history of Seaside Middle School. This game might even be the biggest in the history of middle schools in the entire state of Florida.

After school, Dad and I ran home. Mom had made some pasta in the morning. I knew I needed some carbohydrates in my system. The game was going to be physical and hot, and I needed to prepare my body for a four-quarter battle.

Dad and I didn't say a whole lot before the game.

He was very intense, and so was I. Some players need motivation; some just naturally have it. I had it because Dad had ingrained it into me years ago.

All the preparation and hard work came down to this game.

Game nine was everything a football player could wish for: two undefeated teams. A rivalry and past bad blood also highlighted tonight's game. This game had the making of a Hollywood block-buster movie. When I was younger, I always dreamed of starring in some type of movie or action film.

As a football player, the bright lights and attention around the game added a heightened level of excitement.

This must be what a movie star feels like before the premiere of his or her movie!

Tonight's game wasn't going to be the action movie I had hoped; I would quickly find out that it was turning into a horror film!

-19-

I was short and edgy after school. The anticipation of the game was starting to make me anxious and nervous.

"Are we going to win tonight?" Bubba asked me as we sat on the couch, playing video games.

"Duh! That's the plan," I shot back.

"You're not going to talk to your brother or anyone else like that," Dad said walking into our living room. I was caught off guard as I didn't know he was listening. "Son, don't let your emotions change who you are."

"Dad, I can't believe how calm you are today. I know I don't need to remind you, but tonight is our Seaside," I said.

Dad took a deep slow breath, obviously thinking about what and how he wanted to reply.

"Bruno, this is a huge game, no doubt about it. But guess what? Win or lose, life will go on. Sure, I would much rather win, but if not, the sun will come up tomorrow. Son, it's *just* a football game."

Not in my world it wasn't just a football game; it was so much more. I tried to imagine coming home tonight if we lost to the Seaside Mustangs. I couldn't...even thinking about the scenario brought out anger and frustration. *In no way will I be okay with coming home with a loss tonight.*

Mom was in the kitchen when her cell phone rang. She answered and quickly walked into the living room. "Shut off your video game and turn the television to Channel 2," she said.

I could tell she had a certain sense of urgency in her voice. Without question, I got up, shut off the video game, and tuned to the news channel.

"We are still tracking this storm. The good news is, the storm appears to be heading straight north through the Gulf of Mexico," announced the weatherman. "But if the storm path changes and moves east, Panama City and the surrounding panhandle could be in big trouble.

A look of concern crossed Mom's face.

"Do you think we should play the game tonight?" she asked Dad.

"I don't know, but he said he thinks it's going to miss us," he replied, studying the weather map on the television.

"What do you mean *you don't know?* Dad, we *must* play tonight," I said.

"Son, there are a lot bigger things than playing a football game. I am going to go call Principal McDonald to get his thoughts," replied Dad.

Ten minutes later Dad returned to the living room. "Principal McDonald thinks we are good. He knows some weather people who think Panama City is not going to be in the path of the storm. Plus, he thinks the game will be over well before the storm gets close to the Florida coastline," explained Dad.

I was relieved. The thought of going one more

day without playing Jacoby was too much. We had to play; it was time to show everyone in Florida the South Bay Sharks were for real.

Dad, Bruno, and I left for the game. I was so giddy I could barely sit still on the ten-minute drive to the school. The bus was parked out front, and several of my Shark teammates were already there waiting.

Forty-five minutes later the bus full of hungry Sharks was en route to Hillaker Memorial Stadium. The 25-minute drive seemed to take forever.

As we pulled up to the stadium, it was obvious this wasn't like any other football game I had ever played in.

The parking lot was already packed, and several hundred people were already tailgating. Grills were going, yard games were being played, and a high level of excitement permeated the parking lot. I had never seen tailgating at a junior-high football game—only at high school and college games. Several television crews and media people were already on the field.

Getting off the bus, I glanced over and saw the entire Mustang football team stretching on their custom turf football field. They looked huge.

As we walked toward the field, my eyes searched for him.

I didn't need long to find him. He stood out even among the other giants on his team. Jogging at midfield was Jacoby Howard. Our whole team stopped and stared at him.

He noticed us too. His pace picked up as he started sprinting.

Howard moved with ease and speed; in fact, he moved like no one I had ever seen before. He ran so fast, he looked like a green blur on the horizon. Like a comet streaking through the sky on a dark night, he looked amazing.

-20-

My legs felt like liquid gelatin. I shook each one out, hoping to rid myself of the strange tingling feeling.

"Bruno, don't worry about it. Mine feel the same way," Chet said as he jogged in my direction.

Embarrassed that someone else had noticed how nervous I was, I lowered my head. I was the team leader; I wasn't supposed to show weakness before our biggest game.

We were still a half an hour away from kickoff, and the stadium was already full. Now people were starting to line up around the outer fence of the football field. Several rows of people had already crammed in to watch the game.

The sun was slowly fading on the horizon, casting an eerie shadow over the football field. The stadium lights turned on, illuminating the green turf. The Mustangs' field was immaculate.

Our warm-up routine was always the same, but tonight everything felt different.

"Enjoy that tingle you're feeling. You have worked hard to play in a big game like this. You belong here; we aren't here just to warm up!" Dad yelled as we stretched for calisthenics.

I ran over to grab a drink on the sideline. I was standing there taking a drink of water when I felt Dad's familiar hand on my shoulder. "Son, don't overthink tonight's game. Just react and play fast," he advised.

He added, "We are so proud of you and this football team. One game doesn't change any of that; just go out and give it your all!"

I was as ready as I could ever be.

It was time. For most of the fall season, I had felt like this day would never come. Now that it was here, it almost felt surreal—like a strange dream.

The referees called for the captains, and the three of us jogged out to midfield. We were met by Jacoby Howard and three other Mustangs. All of them looked way older and bigger than we did. I recognized two of the bigger guys from our brief confrontation at the pier.

Our eyes locked, and we stared at each other.

The referee was going over some pregame instructions and rules. Bubba was also there with us. He loved the rules and coin toss. As I have said, he took his job as team manager very seriously.

The referee tossed the coin, and I had called heads. I was relieved when the coin fell gently with heads showing.

"We want the ball!" I said enthusiastically.

"Okay, the Sharks will receive the opening kick-off, and the Mustangs will defend the north goal," said the referee.

After he finished his instructions, he told us to shake hands. I tried to grip each Mustang's hand tightly but quickly realized that they were strong as well.

"We're getting the ball, boys! It's our ball first!" I called, running toward our sideline.

I wanted to set the tempo from the beginning with so much excitement and anticipation in the stadium.

I knew that the longer we had the ball on offense, the better our chances were for keeping it out of Jacoby's hands and for winning the game. Stopping Howard and ball control were going to be the keys to winning this game.

I also knew that we needed to score first. If we didn't start off fast, we would be in trouble against the high-powered Mustang offense.

The horn finally blared, signaling the start of the football game.

We huddled on our sideline around Dad.

"I want everyone to take a deep breath and enjoy this moment. You have earned this. No matter what, go out and act like a Shark tonight!" Dad screamed.

The players roared.

Dad waited for a couple of seconds for the

huddle to come down. "Okay, boys are you ready? We are going to bring the fight to Seaside. Kick-off return team get ready. We are going to run Titan to start the game," said Dad.

Run Titan? I thought.

Did I just hear my dad right?

-21-

Titan was a trick play we had practiced all year but never ran it in a game. The play was complicated and super aggressive, but a lot of things can go wrong when running it.

The huddle was silent as we all stared at Dad. He could sense our apprehension about running Titan.

"Trust me, we have to come out and show them we mean business if we want to stay in this game. My plan will work," my dad said.

Still hesitant about running the play, I spoke up. "Coach, are you *sure* you want to run Titan?" I asked sheepishly.

"Listen, I have watched a ton of game film on

these guys. They are super aggressive and fast; I think we can use that against them on the kickoff return. If we can score on this play, it will set the tempo for the rest of the game," Dad said.

"It will work," Dad said confidently one last time.

My dad had the team's respect, and everyone could tell by the tone of his voice that he believed it, so if he believed then we would too.

"Let's do it!" I said with a huge grin.

Our kickoff return team raced out in our typical formation. The huge crowd had grown even bigger as people were still filing through the main gate.

People were standing along the field because the stands had been filled long ago.

"I can't believe we're going to run Titan right now; this is crazy," I told myself as the Mustang kicker lined up to start the game.

I turned and looked back, glancing at Chet and Leon. They nodded at me. We were ready.

The shrill screech of the referee's whistle officially started the game. The Mustang kicker took his kicking steps and lined up perfectly on the ball.

After a couple of steps, he kicked the football high into the air.

I was one of the middle fullbacks on kickoff returns and the key to start Titan. My job was to catch the ball cleanly and run to my right to make it look like we were returning the ball to the right side of the field.

Time seemed to stand still as I positioned myself under the football and caught it as it made a loud thud into my chest. I turned and took off sprinting to my right.

The Mustangs were flying down the field in my direction.

Dad was right; they were aggressive. Seemingly, all 11 of their kickoff players planned on creaming me as they raced in my direction.

After eight steps, I slowed down and handed the ball to Chet. He had come around the right side and ended up behind me. Our handoff was clean as Chet zoomed toward the left side of the field.

As soon as I handed off the ball, I was clobbered by two Mustang players who hit me so hard, I was thrown down on the unyielding turf, taking my breath away. I rolled over just in time to see Chet being chased by the remaining Mustang players.

With most players from both teams cluttered together on the right side of the field, it left the left side open.

Chet took four more steps and stopped.

The Mustang players started scrambling, realizing what was happening, but it was already too late to do anything.

Chet turned and threw a 30-yard pass behind him to the left sideline to wide-open Leon.

Not a Mustang was close to Leon as he cradled in the perfectly placed pass.

As soon as Leon caught the pass, he turned and started racing down the sideline. No one on the Mustang kickoff team could catch him. The only one with this type of speed was Howard, who was currently standing on the Mustang sideline.

Leon sprinted untouched 80 yards for a Shark touchdown ten seconds into the game. Titan had worked perfectly.

Our home crowd went crazy; the bleachers shook as Leon crossed the end zone. We were the first team to score on the Mustangs in the first half this season.

Our kicker jogged out and booted the extra point, giving us an early 7-0 advantage only 12 seconds into the game!

Taking the lead was a great start but knowing that we could score on Seaside helped take away our initial nervousness and lack of confidence.

Now everyone knew that the Sharks were for real. They knew we weren't there just to warm up.

We came to win.

-22-

Our kickoff team made sure to keep the ball away from Jacoby, who was sitting back deep on their return team. Jacoby had already returned four kickoffs for touchdowns this year, and the last thing we needed was Howard running the kickoff back.

So, our kicker squib kicked it to the middle of the field, and the ball fell short of Jacoby. One of Seaside's players picked it up and was quickly tackled after a short gain.

Our defense rushed onto the field. This was our first time facing a player like Jacoby. I wanted to see how we measured up.

The Mustangs' first play was a run up the middle.

Jacoby handed off the ball to his running back. Leon was spying Jacoby the whole time and stayed with him. I tackled the halfback after a one-yard gain.

On second down, the Mustangs tried a screen pass, but their wide receiver was tackled for a loss of three yards. So far, our defense was outstanding, covering all over the Mustangs. We looked like the faster, more aggressive team.

Seaside had the ball on a third and 12. If we stopped them on this play, they would punt, and we would have done our job by taking the ball out of Jacoby's hands.

But on third down and 12, we got a full introduction to exactly how special of a player Jacoby Howard was.

Jacoby came out in an empty shotgun set with five wide receivers and no running backs. Leon stayed in the middle spying Jacoby and went out wide to cover one of their wide receivers.

Jacoby caught the snap and dropped back to pass. I backpedaled into coverage and covered the flats.

As the running back made his break in front of me, I saw Leon rush toward Jacoby. Howard did an in-and-out move, causing Leon to go airborne and miss him entirely.

Without any wasted motion, Jacoby turned and sprinted down the middle of the field. Once he turned on his speed, he was untouchable. He went untouched 62 yards for a Mustang touchdown. After kicking the extra-point, the game was tied 7-7 with 9:45 left in the first quarter.

The game had barely started, and the offensive fireworks were already going off. I knew this type of game would favor the Mustangs. We weren't built to go back and forth with Seaside. Our defense would need to figure out a way to contain and slow down Jacoby.

The Mustangs kicked off deep to our return man. Titan was the type of play that would only work once. We returned the ball to the 25-yard line as our offense ran onto the field.

As the fullback on our offense, my job was to usually block and make room for the halfback to run. On our first offensive play from scrimmage, I realized this was going to be much tougher than usual. We ran a running play off the right tackle. I led the running back through the hole and met their linebacker at full speed. There was a huge collision as he went through me, tackling our running back in the backfield.

Wow! There is a lot more to this team than just Jacoby, I thought.

The next play was for a loss of one. We tried throwing on third down only to see Chet get sacked for a huge loss. It was fourth and 18 as the punt team ran onto the field.

I thought our offense would be able to move the ball on the Mustangs. I was wrong; their defense was amazing and could hit hard.

We punted, and they signaled for a fair catch on their 40-yard line.

This drive was vital for our defense. It had taken Jacoby just three plays to break off a long run for a touchdown. We had to do much better if we wanted to win this game.

Leon had learned a lot on the first touchdown run. His job wasn't to tackle Jacoby; it was to contain and turn him toward other defenders. He had to bottle him up long enough for others to help; handling Howard would require our entire team.

Leon adjusted and played Jacoby much better on the second drive. Even though the Mustangs drove the ball down the field, they only picked up a couple of first downs. Their second drive lasted a long time, using up several minutes of the clock but also helped our defense regain some of their confidence.

The football game went back and forth in the second quarter as neither team found an advantage.

Then with four minutes remaining in the half, our defense stopped the Mustangs on a third and long play.

The Mustangs went for it on fourth down, but Jacoby's pass was tipped out of his receiver's hands, stopping the drive. Our offense took over deep in their territory.

After a couple of run plays and an incomplete

pass, we faced a fourth and two on the Mustang 24-yard line.

Late in the second quarter, we were tied with the Mustangs. We called our final time out of the first half.

"I think we should go for it," I said to Dad.

Puzzled, he looked at me.

"They don't have any time outs; there will only be enough time for one play, and no matter what, we aren't going to let them score—even if they stop us," I stated.

Dad looked up at the clock, only :04 was left before halftime. If we got the first down, we could manage the clock and go into halftime tied.

Dad agreed and sent the offense back out on the field. The Mustangs were shocked and were already in a punt return formation.

Jacoby, the deep returner, seeing that we were going for it came flying up.

Just as we snapped the ball, he blitzed through the line and tackled our running back at the line of scrimmage, ending our attempt at first down.

With :01 left in the second quarter, the Mustangs had the ball with time for one play before halftime. I quickly knew I had made a mistake by convincing Dad to go for it.

During the time out, something very strange happened. The raucous atmosphere of the game went silent. An eerie calm settled over the field as the wind died down. It was like someone had hit the pause button on the game, and everything just stopped. An odd deafness descended on the stadium.

My stomach turned, and the hair on the back of my neck bristled. The air had shifted, and something was wrong.

What is happening?

-23-

I stood at midfield in a daze.

Seaside called a time out, stopping play. Chet ran up and shook my arm, snapping me back to reality.

I looked toward the Mustang sideline as their kicking team trotted onto the field.

"A field goal?" I said loud enough for Chet and Leon to hear me. We were all in shock as Seaside sent out their place-kicker.

They're lining up for a field goal? I was still searching the sky, trying to make sense of what was happening.

I quickly did the math and figured the attempt would be around 42 yards.

I knew their kicker had a great leg and could kick, but I didn't think he could possibly make a field goal from that distance.

Our defense lined up in a regular defensive formation. "Watch the fake! Watch the fake; I got the holder," I yelled across our defense. In my mind, no way could the kicker hit one from this far.

The ball was snapped, and the holder reached behind as the ball sailed toward his back. He adjusted, made a great catch, and then in one smooth motion, he put the ball down, spinning it so the laces faced our defense. The kicker came through and booted the ball in perfect form.

I turned in both awe and complete shock as the ball flew, rotating end over end and straight through the uprights.

He made it! I can't believe he made it! The entire Seaside sideline went crazy.

Then the unthinkable happened. I will never forget this moment in my life. Just as the football fell behind the goalpost and bounced off the turf, a loud thunderous boom exploded over the field!

At first, I thought someone had set off some fireworks or a cannon. Some schools do that when their team scores, but then I quickly remembered that I hadn't heard anything on Jacoby's first touchdown.

The first boom was followed with one of the biggest, scariest bolts of lightning I had ever seen! The thunder and lightning created instant chaos on the football field.

Players, coaches, and fans alike were running for cover as a torrential downpour started. Our defense took off toward the sideline as other players scrambled for the locker room.

The rain pounded my helmet so hard I could barely see. The sound of more blistering thunder boomed behind me.

The storm isn't going to miss us after all! blasted through my mind.

The entire situation was extremely dangerous. I knew we had to get off the field as quickly as possible! Our sideline was completely empty as I sprinted toward the locker room. I looked up into the bleachers and saw crowds of people scurrying down the steps.

When my foot hit our sideline, a sense of relief flooded over my body. I felt much safer being closer to the locker room and not standing in the middle of the football field.

I glanced back one time to look at the field. I squinted through the downpour to see a small shadow standing frozen on the football field. *Who is that?*

BOOM! An even bigger thunderous roar erupted followed by a huge lightning strike. The brightness of the lightning made me think someone had turned on the football field floodlights.

"Dad, is that you?" I yelled to a figure running from the locker room toward me. The broad shoulders and thick outline quickly revealed it was Coach.

He yelled while heading toward me, "Bubba! Where is Bubba?"

"What about Bubba?" I asked. I was having trouble making out Dad's screams. The rain was hitting my helmet so hard, it sounded like someone was pounding nails into my head.

"Bubba! I can't find Bubba!" shouted Dad.

As Dad reached me, another bolt of lightning flashed, this time hitting the goalpost where the Mustangs had just made the field goal. When it made contact, colorful sparks flew in all directions.

I turned in all directions, frantically looking for Bubba. *Where could he go? Did someone else scoop him up? Was he safe?*

Dad grabbed my arm and pointed at a small shadow near the 30-yard line.

We both realized simultaneously that we were looking at Bubba. Even in all the chaos of the un-folding storm, he was still doing his manager's job—retrieving the kicking tee. Without thinking about the weather, he had sprinted out to retrieve the Mustangs' kicking tee.

Now he was alone and in great danger.

I took off as another bolt of lightning struck near him. I knew that I couldn't make it to him in time. *I'm too slow. The next bolt of lightning is sure to hit my little brother!*

-24-

Dad and I were side by side, sprinting and slipping on the wet turf as we headed toward Bubba.

BOOM! ZAP! Thunder and lightning were everywhere. I had never seen such a ferocious storm in my entire life.

The storm had materialized so quickly, the air around me felt bizarre.

I felt like I was running in mud or quicksand. No matter how fast I ran, it didn't seem like we were getting much closer to Bubba. I knew the next bolt of lightning had the potential to strike Bubba, who was still standing frozen near the 30-yard line.

I was sure he felt scared and lost. Stiff with fear

and disoriented from the massive rainfall, Bubba was a sitting duck for the storm.

BOOM! Thunder erupted, and the reverberating sound was so close, it startled both of us as we ran toward Bubba.

We were still 50 yards from reaching him when a miracle happened. If I hadn't seen it with my own eyes, I wouldn't have believed it.

A figure emerged from the other side of Bubba. Reaching out, he grabbed Bubba and slung him over his shoulder without slowing his sprint.

Once Bubba was safely secured, he seemed to enter warp speed and exploded toward the locker room. Seeing Bubba was now safe, Dad and I both turned and followed.

The person who had Bubba was so much faster than both of us. He was in the locker room when a huge bolt of lightning struck right next to where Bubba had been standing.

Whoever this mystery person was, he had undoubtedly saved my brother's life.

As we entered the crowded locker room, Dad

and I scrambled around looking for Bubba. I scanned around the room filled with players and coaches from both teams.

They all wore the same look—the look of fear.

One of the Seaside players got my attention and pointed toward the back corner of the locker room. I jogged over and found Bubba curled up in the arms of his hero. He was unharmed but terrified. His terrified sobbing broke my heart. I took a deep sigh of relief, knowing he was safe.

"Jacoby, thank you doesn't seem like enough," I said, looking directly into the eyes of my rival and enemy.

Jacoby Howard, with his blazing speed, had unselfishly saved my brother. When everyone else had been running in fear, Jacoby sprinted out to save the ball boy.

"It's all good, Bruno. I just didn't want the little guy to trip again and take a fall," he said with a smile. I knew he was referring to the accident at Pier Park.

His remark even got a smile out of Bubba.

The three of us chuckled briefly.

"Bruno, this isn't good. Something is different about this storm," said Jacoby.

Jacoby's right! Something is very different about this storm.

Little did I know, we were about to experience the strongest hurricane ever to strike the Florida Panhandle. Only the second category 5 hurricane ever to strike the Gulf Coast, Michael had turned to set its sights directly on Panama City. We were all about to feel the wrath of one of the worst hurricanes to ever hit Florida!

-25-

The tropical storm that had looked like it was going to stay west, far away from Panama City, changed direction to set its devastating course directly at the Florida Panhandle, reaching its peak intensity as it hit the Florida coast.

Once everyone was safe and composed, families started to come in and grab their football players. Dad, Bubba, and I stayed until the last player was gone. Mom had already gone home to prepare as best she could for the hurricane.

I knew we weren't out of trouble yet; this was only the beginning. I really wanted to get home.

Home always feels like a safe place.

As we exited the locker room, the dark clouds

took on an evil, ominous look. I stared up into the darkened sky through the pouring rain to see clouds circulating and moving at breakneck speed.

The wind was almost unbearable, blowing so hard we struggled to get to our car. I would find out later wind speeds would hit as high as 129 mph. Once in the car, Dad set the course for our house. Destruction surrounded us everywhere. The streets were eerily empty of cars but covered with trees. I could see power lines swinging in the wind; danger encompassed us.

As we drove down the highway, I felt like the storm was literally following us home. Dad was meticulous and focused on his driving. Everything was dark except our car's headlights; everyone seemed to have lost power, making the drive even spookier.

When we finally made it back to our street, I was shocked. My heart broke as many a house on our block was being torn to shreds. Dog houses and playsets were blowing through our yard as Dad zoomed into the driveway and parked.

Both the wind and the rain were pounding even harder than it had at the football game.

We stumbled into our house, feeling our way along the living room wall. In my parent's room, I saw a small yellow glow. We worked our way toward it, tripping and stumbling over things.

We found Mom hunkered down in their walk-in closet. She had pushed both dressers to the window to help prevent the shattering glass from hurting someone. The look on my mom's face when we walked into the bedroom was one I had never before seen. I saw her immense relief that the three of us had made it home safely. We had no landline phone, cellular service, electricity, or Wi-Fi due to the hurricane.

Mom had collected items we would need and prepared their walk-in closet as a safe zone for the family.

Still shaken from the brute strength of the storm, we all hugged. The wind howled, and the thunder boomed. We could see no evidence of the storm's passing.

Dad put Bubba and me against the wall and shut the closet doors. Mom had lined the closet with couch cushions and blankets. Dad grabbed one of the flashlights from the middle of the closet. He frantically clicked on the button and scanned us. We were crammed in the close quarters, but we were as safe as we could possibly be.

As Dad's light panned the room, a book at my mom's feet was illuminated. Wondering, I grabbed one of the extra flashlights to shine in her in direction. I recognized the old leather-bound book as my mom's Bible, and I noticed it was open to the book of Mark. I could hear her praying and repeating, *"there was a great calm."*

For hours, the storm raged and hammered our house. The four of us sat in a tiny closet, listening to Hurricane Michael tearing apart our neighborhood.

During the night, I lost all track of time. At times, the house would shake, and I worried the roof was gone. After a couple of hours, Bubba finally fell asleep. I guessed it was around 1:00 or

2:00 a.m., but I wasn't sure. I was fighting sleep even though I was so tired from the football game and the drama of the hurricane. Truly, a part of me was afraid to fall asleep. My mind raced with fearful thoughts about the hurricane.

Are my friends and teammates okay?

Were people able to get to safety fast enough?

How many people have lost their lives?

Dad and Mom just stared.

Suddenly, an eerie, quiet calm filled the closet.

"Dad, do you hear that?" I asked.

"No, I don't hear anything," he responded.

"Exactly! It's the first time I don't hear thunder or the howling of the wind," I said.

I quickly added, "Let's go; it's over!"

Dad grabbed my arm and stared. "No, son, it's not over yet. We are in the middle of the storm—in the eye of the hurricane," he said sadly.

The eye of a hurricane is the center of the storm. Inside the eye, everything is calm and normal, but being in the eye is only a short-lived tease. We were only halfway through Hurricane Michael.

Only halfway through this hurricane?

What will the rest of the night hold?

How much more damage will this hurricane cause?

How many more lives would be lost?

The heaviness on my eyelids finally won as I finally fell asleep.

-26-

That night was the longest and worst of my life. Every time I woke up, I found comfort from my parents and their faith. Mom was clutching her Bible, and Dad's steadfast eyes were focused as his arms cradled Bubba.

Every time I woke up and opened my eyes, they were awake. Not one time did they have their eyes closed—not once. I found great comfort in my parents' will to protect us.

I knew they hadn't slept at all the entire night.

Sometime in the early morning hours, I felt some movement near my feet which startled me awake. Dad was getting up from the floor of the closet.

I looked up, wiping the sleep from my eyes.

"Bruno, I think it might finally be over. Stay here!" he said firmly as he slowly opened the closet door.

It's over?

For those living in Panama City, the storm was not over, for the pain from that night would last forever. The residents of our town had little-to-no time to evacuate or prepare. Most just stayed and hunkered down, hoping for the hurricane to end.

The television was down, so our only source of outside communication was a small battery-powered radio Dad pulled out of an old tote from the garage. Dad soon returned to let us know it was safe to leave the closet.

He was sitting in the living room, and the three of us joined him on the floor. The small radio crackled until he found a station that would come in.

The radio station wasn't in Panama City. We would later learn most of them had been destroyed. The radio stations that weren't badly damaged would still take months to be back on the air.

The radio station would later identify itself as one out of Tallahassee. "More than 338,000 people in Florida are without power. Eighteen people have been confirmed dead, and extreme devastation is along the Florida coast," reported the radio newscaster.

We would later find out that the damages would exceed over 8 billion dollars. Hurricane Michael moved its way through Florida before wreaking havoc in Georgia, North Carolina, and Virginia. No other state was as hard hit as Florida.

We sat in the middle of the living room for several minutes nervous, not wanting to open the door and look outside.

Finally, when I couldn't wait any longer, I got up and walked over, opening our front door.

As the door swung open, I couldn't believe my eyes at all the devastation. Houses had been destroyed. The street in front of our house was filled with trees, cars, and other debris. The sight in front of me looked like something out of a war zone.

My hand slipped over my mouth in shock.

The house directly south of us was missing its roof and had been torn in half. Dangerous power lines dangled loosely across several lawns.

I took several steps and turned back to look at our house. To my amazement, ours had suffered very little damage. Several windows had been smashed, our trampoline was missing, and half of our roof was missing shingles. In comparison to our neighbors, we were lucky as most of our house had been spared. Most of our neighborhood looked like someone had taken a wrecking ball through it, smashing everything in its way.

The rest of my family joined me as we walked down the street to see if anyone needed help. People were starting to leave their houses—shaken but thankful to be alive.

We kept walking toward the end of our street. I noticed a large group of people had gathered to stare toward the entry to the local beach.

We walked toward them, but I wasn't prepared for what I saw next.

The beautiful beaches, the ones that drew so

many people to Panama City, were torn apart. The power of the hurricane had ripped through, destroying the beautifully groomed beach, and tearing down the neighboring pier.

It even destroyed the beaches? I thought.

"Damaged, yes, but not destroyed," said Dad.

Little did I know the extent of Hurricane Michael. Visually, I could see mayhem and devastation, but the damage was on a much larger scale than we could see.

That day, the President of the United States issued an emergency declaration for the state of Florida.

What had started as a tropical storm turned into one of the worst hurricanes on record, lasting nine days before eventually weakening over Georgia and ending in the Atlantic Ocean.

In less than 12 hours, Hurricane Michael had managed to destroy a large part of my hometown.

-27-

The days following the hurricane were spent helping and serving others. During the daytime, neighbors helped neighbors; our entire block worked together to clean and repair our homes.

With so much debris, traveling in a car was nearly impossible. We walked everywhere. No businesses or restaurants were open; after six days we would finally have consistent electricity.

The days that followed were sad, but we began to see small, hopeful signs of better days. The entire world had seemingly stopped with all the usual crazy busyness of life gone. It was time to rebuild our town and our hearts.

Some good things happened during this time

of rebuilding a city. The food was all homecooked and amazing. Our evenings were filled with laughter and fun. With cell phones and Wi-Fi still down, we had to find other ways to pass the time. One of the best ways was the board games and fun we had at night. We sat around campfires telling stories.

During this time, I realized I had never been so close to my neighbors. We had some I had never even taken time to talk to. After a couple of days together, our whole block was becoming like family.

Out of the darkness and carnage, a small light flickered with hope within the community blocks and streets in Panama City.

Healing can be a tricky process; sometimes the only true thing that heals is time. Some events are so tragic and hurt so deeply, that even time can't even totally heal.

Hurricane Michael had destroyed everything I loved—my school, my neighborhood, and football.

Even though most of our house was spared, South Bay was not. Hurricane Michael hit our school hard, with ferocity and the unwavering power only generated by a hurricane.

When the roads were finally safe, Dad and I drove to the school. The building was a sad sight. Complete sections of the roof were missing. The huge glass windows in the front of the school were blown out. Glass and pieces of metal were strewn all over the campus. The baseball and softball dugouts had been torn from their foundations and slammed into the basketball gym.

Our football field had been destroyed. Both goalposts were missing, and we had no idea what had happened to them. The bleachers had blown over, crashing onto the field, and gouging a huge hole in the turf at the 50-yard line.

The once bright-green grass was now a pale brown. The sprinkler system had been damaged, and the bright Florida sun had scorched the field. The lack of water had killed the grass in a short time. Dad was trying to be brave, but I could see the disappointment in his eyes as he looked at a field he had spent so much time perfecting.

" All of this can be rebuilt…" Dad muttered just loud enough for me to hear him but not loud enough to convince me that he believed it.

The most shocking damage was to our beaches. Panama City beaches are some of the most beautiful in the world. As we drove by Pier Park, I saw that most of it was gone. The beach was unrecognizable. Instead of seeing white, gorgeous rolling sand, we saw a beach covered in trash and debris. Instead of sand volleyball and people sunbathing, the beach was filled with what was left of houses, vehicles, and trash.

"Will we be able to go back to school?" I asked my dad.

Most of the time, we were looking for ways to miss school or get a day off. I didn't have those feelings. Instead, I felt like we needed school more than ever, but I didn't see a way we would be able to go back to South Bay with all the damage.

"Son, I don't…I just don't know," Dad answered in a somber voice.

-28-

As another week passed, the rest of the world was already forgetting about Hurricane Michael. The category 5 storm was no longer on every news channel or the talk of the country. The media was now fixated on the Ebola virus in the Congo of Africa. The tragedy of Hurricane Michael was left for those living the nightmare; the rest of the world had moved on.

As improvements were made, some things started to return to normal. We finally had power again, which was great for taking a shower and having a fridge again.

But something weird had happened. Even though we had electricity and our cell phones were working again, we still met at night with our neighbors. The games and fun we had enjoyed in the evenings still mattered to all of us. Our street had changed; we had become a caring, community of neighbors.

Even in the tragedy, a lot of good resulted from the hurricane. Bubba and I had grown much closer. The hurricane helped me realize how precious every day was.

I was thankful when our church reopened, and I got to see a lot of my friends and teammates from South Bay. None of my teammates had been injured, but several had lost their homes.

Slowly, through community effort and hard work, the town of Panama City started to recover.

Three weeks after Hurricane Michael, my dad received a phone call from our principal. He explained that we were going to try to resume school in another week. South Bay School was too damaged to attend, so our school had come up with a revised schedule. Each school in our district was scrambling to find buildings that could provide makeshift classrooms and get kids back to some type of schedule.

Our middle school students would start school at a huge library that was two miles from our school. The library had several buildings and abundant space. The staff at South Bay had spent the past week moving chairs and desks, setting up classrooms. Fortunately, the hurricane had skirted the library, making it the best place to get us back into school.

I had never been so excited to return to school.

Four weeks after the category-5 hurricane ravaged our town, I was sitting back in Mr. Moats' math class next to Chet in a small room in the back of the library. I was shocked at how thankful everyone was to be back. Kids wanted to learn; no one was talking when the teacher was talking. Obviously, the tragedy had given my classmates a new perspective—one of gratitude.

While much of the Florida Panhandle had been demolished, human connection and a belief in each other hadn't been destroyed or weakened.

At the end of math class, Chet leaned in close to me. "Do you think we would have won?" he whispered innocently.

At first, I was confused and shot him a baffled look.

"The game, Bruno! Do you think we had a shot?" he asked again.

The football game versus the Seaside Mustangs was a distant memory. I hadn't thought about it one time in the past four weeks—not once. My world had changed so much, and I had been in survival mode.

But…Chet's question intrigued me.

I wonder what would have happened if we could have finished that game? We were in good shape only being down 10-7 at halftime. Could we have pulled off the impossible?

I looked at Chet and shrugged my shoulders.

"I guess we will never know," I said sadly.

-29-

If I had learned anything from the tragic events of Hurricane Michael, it was to value your faith and family. Looking back, I can see where I had put football in front of both. While mine had been a tough lesson, I knew that I would never again make the same mistake.

The entire day, Chet's words kept running through my mind. I replayed the first half of the game in my mind. I thought how they were fast and an amazing team, but so were we. As I walked around school, I noticed a heavy sense of sadness. Even though kids were happy to be back together, a dark cloud was hanging over our heads. The doldrums were still noticeable the next day and the next.

By Friday, I had to say something. I waited for Chet and Leon to sit next to me at one of the picnic tables we were using for lunch.

"Does everyone seem sad to you?" I asked.

Without hesitating, Leon responded, "I feel it too, man. I know the storm was tough, but everyone has this hopeless look on their face."

"I agree with both of you guys. It's almost like we have nothing to look forward to. Thanksgiving and Christmas are too far away. I know it's nice to be back in school, but it's still…well, school," said Chet.

He had made a good point. Most of the businesses in town were still closed. The beaches were still cluttered and unsafe.

"What is there to look forward to? What would add some excitement and make people smile again?" I asked.

"What can we really do? I mean just get through the day, I guess," said Leon.

His statement was probably what most of the kids and their families were feeling in Panama City; they were all hoping to get through the day.

Having no hope is a depressing, sad feeling. Our community needed something to smile about again. I closed my eyes, asking for a sign or an idea of what we could do to make the kids in Panama City smile again.

I slowly opened my eyes, expecting a flashing neon sign that would give me an answer. The neon sign wasn't there, and I got up from lunch hopeful something positive would come up soon.

My mind raced and wandered all day trying to think of what we could do to help everyone. The more I thought about it, the more my mind wandered and raced with ideas. We could do a concert and bring in a big-name performer who was sure to make people smile. Then I remembered that money was a problem, and we had nowhere for them to perform. Plus, I didn't know any famous singers.

I had a ton of ideas—everything from selling oranges to cookies to all the fundraisers we had done in the past. But I didn't think asking people for money or to make cookies would make people smile again.

I was starting to get upset at myself for not being

able to come up with any good ideas. Then as in most cases, my thoughts started to turn negative.

"It's not really my job to do this anyway. I am just a kid; I'm sure other people are working on it," I told myself. *I don't know anyone famous, I have zero money, and all that I really know anything about is football. I'm not the right person to solve this problem.*

When I thought those negative thoughts, my mind flashed to all the selfless helpers I had met during the aftermath of the hurricane. I saw complete strangers volunteering and stepping up. People in my community were constantly putting other people's needs in front of their own.

That was community; that was my town. I knew the right thing to do was to be one of the helpers—one of the problem solvers. The wheels were already in motion, and I was about to be part of something much bigger than I ever imagined.

With ten minutes left before lunch on Friday, a loudspeaker went off. The crackling noise startled me. The sound system at the library was old and outdated—nothing like the one we had at South Bay.

I recognized the voice right away; it was Mr. Mc-Donald, the principal.

"Bruno Barnes to the office, please," he said as the speakers boomed.

-30-

Office? I wasn't sure where the office was at the library as I wondered around lost. Finally, after a couple of minutes, I heard some people talking in a back office near the fiction section.

I walked toward the voices and saw Mr. McDonald's secretary sitting behind a picnic table. She looked up from her work and pointed toward another door at the back of the room. I thanked her and then heard a familiar voice.

"Welcome, Bruno! Come on in. I would like to share something with you," said Mr. McDonald.

I was still confused at why I was being called to the office. Mr. McDonald was usually quite upbeat, but I could tell by the tone of his voice that he had something important on his mind. "Bruno, I got a surprise phone call this morning from Seaside's principal, Mr. Martinez," he said.

Why would Seaside be calling South Bay?

"He had a great idea," he said. I nodded intently, interested to hear what his idea was.

"Seaside wants to finish the second half of our football game that the hurricane ended," explained Mr. McDonald.

I sat in shock, not knowing what to say next. The idea of completing our game had never crossed my mind. I knew our field was out of the question, and I had heard that Seaside had been hit as hard as we were. Plus, I didn't think anyone would be in the mood to watch a junior-high football game.

He added, "Our community needs something, Bruno. Everyday feels sad and hopeless. Our school and our entire community is still healing. Maybe we could give them a small reason to smile."

"But where? How?" I mumbled, still in shock from his unexpected news.

"That's the beauty of it. I made some calls today,

and Gulf Coast State College has agreed to host the game," he explained.

Gulf Coast State College was a community college located in Panama City. This junior college would be less than a 20-minute drive for both schools. Mr. McDonald went on to explain how most of the campus was in great shape, and he knew some people there. They were more than happy to host the game.

"Do you think playing a second half of junior-high football game will help anyone?" I asked.

"I don't know, Bruno, but it's something. An event like this might bring people together even more," he said.

"When do they want to play?" I asked.

"I think this could be good for you and your team. This school sure could use something uplifting right about now," he said, acting like he didn't hear my question.

"I agree, but when do they want to play?" I asked again.

I could tell he was trying to get me to commit

to our team playing the game. He went on to say more as I sat and stared.

He stopped talking and looked at me. He knew I was waiting for an answer to my question.

"That's the interesting part. If this is going to happen, it must happen soon," he said.

"Okay, how soon?" I quickly replied.

"Like Sunday soon," he said.

"In two days—this Sunday?" I asked in shock.

He nodded, and I shrunk in my chair. Our team isn't ready mentally or physically to play the Mustangs. We would be fortunate if we could even get the guys around in time to play in two days.

Mr. McDonald went on to tell me that Sunday was the only date that worked for all three schools. He also mentioned that per Florida rules, a game must be made up and completed within 30 days of the original start date.

We had no choice if we wanted to finish the game. Having some closure to see if we really had what it takes to beat the Mustangs would be nice. Our town needed something to pick up their spirits.

I knew in my heart he was right. We all needed to finish second half of the Sharks versus Mustangs game. More was at stake than two undefeated football teams.

The entire town of Panama City needed this game.

-31-

Word spread quickly, and a football meeting was scheduled during our last hour of school. The players met in the gym, and Dad was ready to present our option about playing Seaside on Sunday.

At first, our team had mixed feelings.

"Coach, we aren't ready. I haven't put on my cleats since the night of the hurricane," responded one of our linemen.

"We could lose, but I like the fact that we are still undefeated and technically didn't lose to Seaside," said another player.

Dad listened intently and never interrupted. After everyone had a chance to speak, I felt like it was my turn to say something.

"Guys, I really feel like playing the second half of this game must happen. This game has nothing to do with us or Seaside. This game is for the people of Panama City. Everyone needs something to smile about again," I said.

"How will this help?" asked an eighth grader.

"I want you to all close your eyes and think. When was the last time you really smiled or your parents looked happy? I can only speak for myself, but the last time I smiled was the night of our last game—before the storm," I said.

The wheels were turning, and my teammates were looking around at each other. It clicked for them. If anything, this game would give everyone a break from the hurricane and provide a moment of relief everyone desperately needed.

"I'm in," said Chet

"Me too," agreed Leon.

"With a show of hands, who is in favor of finishing our game with Seaside on Sunday?" Dad asked.

In unison, the rest of the team raised their hands; they all agreed to play.

"Okay, Sunday at 2:00 p.m., we will finish our game with the Mustangs," Dad announced.

We quickly planned on having one practice on Saturday to walk through plays and get used to the turf at the stadium. Dad knew that two hours wouldn't be enough to prepare for Seaside, but it was better than nothing at all.

By the time school was dismissed, a buzz was growing about the game. The atmosphere at school wasn't so somber. The hallways were a tad louder, and kids seemed to have more energy.

The kids now had something to look forward to. It seemed like the first time everyone had a reason to smile again since the hurricane.

On our way home, I noticed several houses had displayed their South Bay Sharks flags again. The secret was out of the bag, and our town was preparing for a football game once again.

I was proud to be a South Bay Shark and proud to be from Panama City—at least what was left of our city. The hurricane had destroyed so much of our beloved city, but it hadn't taken away our heart.

-32-

Saturday's football practice was interesting. A huge sense of excitement came with being back on the football field.

For four weeks, I had thought my football season had ended. Now we had one more chance— one more half of a football game left in our season. I was out of shape. I felt slow, and everything on my body seemed out of sync. It wasn't just me. Our team didn't look the same as it did before the hurricane.

The stadium at Gulf Coast State College was awesome and in great shape. I couldn't help but think how fast Jacoby would be on this turf.

During a water break, Leon approached me.

"Did you hear the news?" he asked.

"What news?" I replied.

"Dude, it's all over social media. Jacoby is transferring to some big prep school down by Miami for high school. And it looks like he has already moved out of Panama City," said Leon.

He added, "A bunch of players from Seaside are saying he won't be playing tomorrow."

No! That can't happen! Jacoby Howard has to play tomorrow. If he doesn't, I will never know if I have what it takes to stop him.

After practice, I approached one of our assistant coaches, Coach Biz. He lived near Seaside and knew a lot of the player on their team.

"Coach Biz, what's this I'm hearing about Howard?" I asked.

"I am hearing it too. Heard he might already be on his way to Miami," he said shaking his head.

"He has to play! We need to finish this thing," I said.

"I feel that too. I am going to give his dad a call; he's an old buddy of mine," he said.

"Please," I said staring at him.

"Oh, you mean like now. You want me to call him right now?" he asked.

I nodded. *I'm not going home until I know.*

He pulled out his cell phone and walked out of the locker room.

Five minutes later he walked back in with a huge smile on his face.

"You got your wish, Bruno. Jacoby will be there in uniform tomorrow. He's playing," he said.

I smiled. Our paths were meant to meet one more time on the football field.

That night at dinner I barely ate. I sat flipping my spaghetti with my fork. I was so excited and anxious, I couldn't eat.

"You better eat; you will need your energy. That Jacoby is fast, and I should know," said Bubba. I smirked at him, knowing he was referring to Howard's saving him from the hurricane.

He added, "I am going to ask him for his autograph at the game."

I shot him a stare. "No little brother of mine is

asking that Seaside quarterback for an autograph,"
I snarled at him.

Bubba shot his tongue out at me, annoyed at my
harsh response.

*I don't need any more reminders of how awesome
Jacoby Howard is.*

Dad got up and walked into the kitchen to clear
off his plate. Bubba, Dad's constant shadow, quickly followed behind him.

Mom and I were the only ones left at the table.

She had something on her mind and was waiting for the right time. I knew she figured now was
the right time.

"Bruno, you know we are really proud of you.
I know you are excited about the game tomorrow.
But in the end, it's just a football game," said Mom.
After everything Panama City had been through
with Hurricane Michael, just a football game was
what our city needed. My will to win or to stop
Jacoby Howard hadn't changed, but my perspec-
tive had.

"No, Mom, tomorrow isn't just a football game.

———

This game is going to give everyone time to relax and enjoy being together again."

I thought, *so much had changed over the past four weeks, but one thing that hadn't changed was the joy this game was going to bring our community.*

Joy was something Panama City needed now more than ever.

That night I slept great and was the first night in a long time that I didn't have any nightmares. My mind was clear, and I was thankful.

The next day I knew our football game was going to happen, putting an end to our rivalry with Seaside.

———

-33-

When I woke up Sunday morning, the sun was shining bright in a clear, blue sky. *What a beautiful morning!*

The game was scheduled to start at 4:00 p.m., so we had plenty of time to head toward the football stadium after church.

Today's game day had a much different feel than the first time we had played Seaside. I couldn't really explain why, but I felt like everything was going to be good.

On our way to the football game, I saw small signs that Panama City was going to be okay. Most of the debris and destruction caused by Hurricane Michael had been removed. While it wasn't perfect or like it used to be, our city looked way better than it had four weeks ago. Our town had hope again; we knew better days were ahead.

Exactly how many people were excited for the game? More than I could have ever imagined...

I wasn't prepared when we pulled off the expressway and exited toward the stadium. The road was filled with signs and people, cheering our bus as we slowly rolled by. The half-mile drive was lined with fans and supporters. I knew more people were there than from just our two schools. It had seemed like the entire town of Panama City had showed up to cheer us on and watch a football game.

The hair on the back of my neck stood on end, and goosebumps filled my arms.

As we pulled into the stadium, the flow of people increased. The entire parking lot was filled, and people were everywhere. The atmosphere was like something out of a movie.

My skin tingled as we stepped off the bus to a loud roar of applause. The players couldn't contain their grins as we walked into the locker rooms to get dressed.

"This is crazy! I can't believe how many people are here," Leon said.

"Yeah, all for a football game?" I said in a questioning manner.

"Nah, man, this isn't about a football game; this is about life. This is about Panama City's letting everyone know that even though we were down and out, we didn't quit. This is much bigger than any old football game," Chet said.

I couldn't help but think about Chet's words as I got dressed. This game was about so much more than just football. Even though I loved the game, some would even say I was obsessed by it. But the more I thought about it, no game is bigger than the game of life.

Our focus was on people and relationships; they become a priority over things.

It didn't matter if you were a Mustang or a Shark. Today, Panama City was a city of champions!

-34-

By game time, the stands were full and only standing room remained.

During our first meeting, the halftime score was 10-7 in favor of the Mustangs. They had the lead and were receiving the second half opening kickoff.

I would later find out that this was the first football game played after Hurricane Michael within 200 miles of Panama City.

That we were even able to play was a gift.

I get a certain feeling whenever I walk onto the football field. It's hard to explain with words. I feel nervous, anxious, scared, and confident all at once. How ever I describe this feeling, nothing gives me the same feeling I get right before a football game. I love every ounce of it.

The crowd roared as we kicked off and sprinted downfield toward the Mustang return man. Ours was a booming kick, and the receiver signaled a fair catch around the 20-yard line.

Our defense was up first. I took the huddle with my chin held high.

"Boys, today we roll with each other through the good and the bad. I am proud of every one of you. Sharks forever!" I yelled as we broke the huddle for the first play.

We lined up with Leon still spying on Jacoby. I watched as their team shifted into the shotgun. I adjusted and widened out in the flat. Howard snapped the ball to his halfback next to him. I blitzed and almost took the handoff from Jacoby before blowing up the running back with a huge hit.

The crowd roared.

The next play Jacoby faked and kept the ball, sweeping to his left. He was met by Leon after a short gain. So far, we looked prepared to finish the second half of the game just as we had started the first game, by flying around and not letting the Mustangs' speed and size intimidate us.

It was third and seven and looked like our offense was about to get the football. All we had to do was hold them on this third down, and we would get the football back.

Jacoby dropped back and started running to his right. I came flying up and so did Leon. The play was designed to look like it was a quarterback run. Just as we were about to have a huge collision with Howard, he stopped and fired the ball deep down the field.

What an arm! Not only was Howard an unbelievable runner, but he had an elite arm. I had never seen someone throw such a long, perfect spiral.

This kid is a superstar!

The backside tight end had started out blocking before slowly leaking down the field wide open. Howard's pass hit his receiver in perfect stride for a 77-yard touchdown pass. The Mustangs took a 17-7 lead early in the third quarter.

The next two possessions were like a chess game. Neither defense gave up many yards, and both teams were forced to punt.

We received the ball back with 1:39 remaining in the third quarter. Their massive size on the defensive line was starting to wear us down.

The Sharks had the ball on the Mustang 30-yard line. Dad decided to try a pass on first down, but Chet got sacked before he could even get into a three-step drop.

The Mustang defense was fast and aggressive. On second down, Chet handed me the ball where I was quickly met in our backfield behind the line of scrimmage.

"I got an idea," Chet said as I returned to the huddle. "Listen, let them get through the line free; don't touch them. Leon, I want you to run like you are blocking and then turn around. I am going to hit you with the ball in the middle behind our linemen. It should be wide open."

One of our linemen spoke up. "You want us not to block them?" he questioned.

Chet grinned. "Yeah, basically let them through like you have been this whole game," he said with a laugh.

The entire offense chuckled as they broke the huddle.

Chet lined up, and when the ball was snapped, chaos erupted. All five linemen pass rushed along with both linebackers. The Mustangs had called an all-out blitz. Chet sprinted back and looked to be in big trouble.

Right before he was destroyed by a host of Mustang defenders, he jumped in the air and dropped off a perfect pass to our running back.

He caught it just as the linemen exploded up the field. We had five of our guys versus just their two safeties.

It was over! Leon caught the ball and was free for a 70-yard touchdown untouched as the third quarter horn blew.

Mustangs 17, Sharks 14…heading into the fourth quarter.

-35-

The fourth quarter was setting up for an epic finish. The fans were getting all they had hoped for and more. The game had been played well by both teams. Everyone was watching, wondering who was going to make the next big play.

Dad and I had watched a ton of film of the Mustangs, and as the defensive captain, I had tried to memorize their formations and plays. That dedication and time spent watching film was about to pay off in a big way.

With 3:12 remaining in the fourth quarter, the Mustangs came out in shotgun formation with one running back to the right of the quarterback. The pattern was nothing new; they had run this play often.

What caught my attention was the outside receivers lining up in a stack formation. Then the running back went in motion toward the double receivers' side of the field. I now knew exactly what play they were running.

I ran up and acted like I was going to blitz the quarterback, making sure Jacoby saw me.

The center snapped the ball, and Jacoby looked to his right and toward the three receivers' side.

Instead of blitzing, I backpedaled and found the backside tight end.

Howard dropped back and pump faked toward the right before turning back left to hit the tight end who was running a streak up the field.

I timed it perfectly and started my break just as Jacoby let go of the ball. By the time I got to the tight end, I was at a full sprint. I reached out extending my arms as high as they would go.

I felt the hard football slam into my fingertips as I intercepted the pass right before reaching his receiver's hands. Howard was in shock and had no idea I had dropped back into pass coverage.

I was already streaking down the sideline before he realized I had intercepted the ball. Jacoby dug his cleats in and took off sprinting at seeming Mach speed for me. I turned once to see a flash of his jersey closing in on me.

Howard zoomed down the field, running faster than any man I had ever seen. My lungs started to burn, and I felt a cramp starting to develop in my right calf. I pushed on, but I knew that I was drastically slowing down. I set my eyes on the upcoming orange pylon and sprinted with all that I had left. I felt Howard's hit before I saw him. As soon as the contact hit me, I jumped airborne straight toward the goal line.

I landed with a loud thud and the force of the blow knocked the wind out of me. I rolled over in time to see the official holding up his arms, signaling a touchdown.

After a successful extra point, the Sharks took only our second lead of the game, 21-17 with fewer than three minutes remaining in the game.

The touchdown run had taken a lot out of me

physically. As I got mobbed by my teammates, I thought back to those hot summer days of running and training for this exact moment in history. All that work was for this moment, and it was worth every second of it!

For the first time ever, the Sharks looked like they were going to beat the Mustangs. All we needed to do was keep them out of the end zone in the next couple of minutes. A field goal wouldn't do; they had to score.

I grabbed a water bottle out of the Bubba's hands as I jogged over to the sideline. Our eyes met, and we had a special moment as he looked at me the way that he had looked at Jacoby.

He was proud of me, honored to be my brother. His smile beamed from ear to ear.

That was my moment. My brother looked at me like he had looked at Jacoby the night his hero had saved him from the storm. I knew right then and there that my dream had come true. I was now my brother's hero!

-36-

If the Mustangs were going to beat us, they were going to have to do it the hard way, and time wasn't on their side.

I watched the clock as each second ticked away, bringing us closer to a huge victory over unbeaten Seaside.

Jacoby was still making amazing plays, but putting Leon on him helped slow him down. Twice on the drive, Howard almost broke free and would have been gone if it wasn't for a shoestring tackle by Leon.

The Mustangs were moving the ball down the field, taking time off the clock as they were getting closer and closer to the end zone.

I started to get worried when the Mustangs cracked within the ten-yard line.

The Mustangs called their second time out, leaving them with only one remaining. It was third down on the nine-yard line with only :12 seconds remaining in the game.

"We got this boys!" I yelled. I figured they had two plays left in the game. If we didn't let Jacoby loose, they wouldn't be able to score.

"You good?" I asked, looking over at Chet. He looked tired but nodded confidently.

The Mustangs broke the huddle, and Howard called the cadence. The ball was snapped to Jacoby who started running to his right before handing the ball off to the running back. Once the ball was traded off, I took off for the running back. I got so caught up in the rush of the game, I wasn't thinking straight. I roared toward the running back just as he stopped to throw the ball all the way back to a wide-open Howard.

My heart stopped as Howard caught the ball cleanly. He had the entire side of the field wide open for a sure Mustang touchdown. I turned to run toward the goal line, knowing I had to take the right angle to even have a chance at stopping him. I sprinted with every ounce of energy I had left only to see him race past me.

All looked lost as Jacoby ran for what looked like a sure touchdown. I looked up and watched as the clock ticked down, :06, :05, and watched in disbelief, knowing I had fallen for the trick play. I wasn't even thinking about a halfback pass. I should have known better.

Then a miracle happened.

Out of nowhere a blue jersey streaked past me and collided with Jacoby just as he was diving into the end zone. I kept running staring at the referee, but no touchdown signal was given.

The force of the whistle stopped me in my tracks.

"Time out! Time out, Mustangs," said the official in a booming voice. I looked up at the clock to see it now read :03. The ball was inches from the goal line, but Howard was short of the goal line.

———

Leon had saved the game-winning touchdown by tackling Jacoby as he was about to cross the goal line.

The game, our season, was going to come down to one play. Howard was inches away from a touchdown and winning the game. It wasn't just fourth and inches; it was fourth and forever.

This one play would live on in Panama City history forever!

———

-37-

The wild, rowdy crowd suddenly went quiet. In fact, everything around me did.

There was no background noise any longer; it was only Jacoby Howard and me on the goal line. The giant stadium suddenly didn't feel so big. My eyes narrowed, and I had tunnel vision. I don't even remember calling the defensive play. My eyes were fixed on Jacoby's, and his eyes returned my stare.

The Mustangs broke the huddle and lined up in a tight formation. The entire stadium knew where the ball was going. I knew where it was going.

I walked up and stood in the gap between the center and the guard. A quarterback sneak was inevitable, and I had picked one side while Chet picked the other. I knew I had to time it exactly right to stop Jacoby. I crouched, lowering my body ready to surge forward.

The center slowly moved the ball, snapping it back to the quarterback. As soon as he lifted his hand, I rushed in. The center tried to step in my way to slow me down, but he was too slow. I stayed low and dropped my shoulder pads just in time to meet Jacoby at the line of scrimmage.

We connected with a loud thud on impact. He was stronger than I had thought. I wrapped my arms around his waist driving and pushing toward the turf. The window to tackle him was so small, I knew I had to win the initial contact.

I drove my legs as he pushed, and we both finally fell to the ground. I rolled over and looked toward Jacoby. He was lying on top of me, and the ball was stretched out as he reached for the end zone.

Short! He was short! I jumped up and started running toward our sideline celebrating.

We had done it! We had beaten the Seaside Mustangs!

As I sprinted toward the sideline, I noticed that no one else was celebrating. I slowed down and turned around to look back at our defense.

I couldn't believe what I saw...

A yellow flag was lying on the field directly behind some of our defensive players standing with their heads lowered. Instantly, I knew the penalty was on us. The referee signaled offside on the defense as all the Mustangs celebrated. One of our defensive linemen was so amped up, he had crossed the neutral zone early before the snap.

No time was left on the clock, but the game couldn't end on a defensive penalty. The referee slowly moved the football one inch closer.

Seaside would have one more play left and another chance to win the game. I jogged back to our huddle with my head down in disbelief.

"Chin up, captain! We can do this. You stopped him once; you can stop him again," said Leon.

While I appreciated Leon's trying to be positive,

I knew that he was wrong. I didn't have anything left; I had given everything I had on the last play.

The referees spotted the ball, and I lined up one last time.

This time the snap happened lightning fast; Jacoby grabbed the ball, dove into the pile, and stretched for the goal line. By the time I got my bearings, the Mustangs had already scored the winning touchdown.

The Mustangs celebrated as we walked over to our sideline.

We were crushed that we had been so close but lost. Walking off the field, I realized this was the last time that I would play with some of my friends. The South Bay Sharks were undefeated no more.

I looked at Chet, and he shot me his quirky grin. "We battled, Bruno. No doubt Seaside will remember the Sharks," he said.

I don't remember a lot about my dad's pep talk after the game except he was proud of us and our effort. I gave Leon and Chet a big hug and thanked them for being my best friends. We all teared up a bit, knowing our season was over.

The football field started to clear, and most of the people had already left the stadium. I was having trouble taking off my pads. I just didn't want my year to end.

Dad walked up and looked me directly in my eyes and smiled. "Take your time, son. This is your moment," he said.

Hurricane Michael had taught me several valuable lessons. One I had learned was there are more important things in life than football. Hurricane Michael taught me to believe there is good in people. I saw it all the time in the days following the hurricane.

I knew I would replay the goal-line play in my mind millions of time.

I had met the great Jacoby Howard and gave him everything I had. I had won the initial battle, but Howard and his Mustang teammates won the war.

We may not have won the game, but that was okay. I knew there would be more fourth downs, touchdowns and football games in the future.

The game of football meant so much to me, I was glad that for a short time on a Sunday afternoon we could use the game to give something back to our town.

Smiling broadly, Bubba ran up holding a football. "What a hit that was, Bruno! Jacoby Howard will never forget you!"

"Thanks, little brother."

He took two steps back and pulled a black Sharpie marker from his back pocket. With pride in his eyes, he looked up at me and motioned for me to take the Sharpie.

I knew immediately what he wanted.

I smiled as I signed my name on the football.

My brother wants my autograph.

He turned and started running toward my dad, cradling his football like he was holding a million dollars.

As Bubba jogged away, I noticed some additional black writing on the other side of the football.

#13 Jacoby Howard...

Bubba had finally gotten his autograph. This time I wasn't jealous; I was just content to have my name on the same football as Jacoby.

As I watched Bubba bounding off, I felt a forceful hand on my shoulder. I turned around to see the entire Mustang football team standing behind me.

I recognized two of the biggest Mustang football players right away from the incident at the pier. I was by myself and alone without any reinforcements. I stepped back, not knowing what to expect.

One of the big linemen extended his hand and shook mine with a simple, respectful nod. Then, one by one, all the other Mustangs filed through, shaking my hand.

I was in shock that so many players had stayed after the game to show me respect. One by one they went by, with each firmly shaking my hand until only one lone player remained. Jacoby sauntered toward me.

There we were, just the two of us standing alone in the middle of the football field.

"Bruno, I have never been hit like that in my life. You got some serious game, man! I have nothing but respect for you," he said, wrapping his long arms around me as we hugged.

"Good luck, man. Thanks for showing me what a real superstar looks like," I said.

Jacoby smiled and jogged off toward a crowd waiting for him. I started walking toward the locker room when I heard Howard's voice.

"Bruno!" he yelled across the field.

I turned.

"Better tell your brother not to sell that ball. Could be worth a lot of money someday. It might be the only football to have the autographs of two future Hall of Famers on it!"

About the Author

Lane Walker is an award-winning author, educator and highly sought-after speaker. Walker started his career as a fifth grade teacher before transitioning into educational administration, serving as a highly effective principal for over 12 years. He has coached football, basketball and softball.

Lane paid his way through college working as a news and sports reporter for a newspaper. He grew up in a hunting-and-fishing fanatical house, with his owning a taxidermy business.

After college, he combined his love for writing and the outdoors. For the past 20 years, he has been an outdoor writer, publishing over 250 articles in newspapers and magazines. Walker's Hometown Hunters Collection won a Moonbeam Bronze Medal for Best Book Series Chapter Books. His second series, The

Fishing Chronicles, won a Moonbeam Gold Medal for Best Book Series Chapter Books.

Lane launched a brand-new, sports-themed book collection called Local Legends in the spring of 2022.

Stay tuned! More exciting chapter books by Lane will be released in the future!

Visit:
www.bakkenbooks.com

Made in the USA
Monee, IL
13 September 2022

13928360R00105